LIFE EVERLASTING

Il ciclo degli ultimi:

THE FIFTH ESTATE
LIFE EVERLASTING
MEMORIAL

TMP

Ferdinando Camon

LIFE EVERLASTING

Translated by John Shepley

THE MARLBORO PRESS
MARLBORO, VERMONT

First English language edition

Originally published in Italian as
LA VITA ETERNA

The publication of the present volume is made possible by a grant from the National Endowment for the Arts.

Manufactured in the United States of America

Library of Congress Catalog Card Number 87-81085

Cloth: ISBN 0-910395-31-4
Paper: ISBN 0-910395-32-2

To Jean-Paul Sartre,
critical conscience
of the twentieth century.

Contents

Preface

Among the novels I have written, *Life Everlasting* is the one that contradicts the others: it tells the story of the rebellion of a people that did not want to rebel. A people wont to live quietly, to work, pray, and endure, the most perfect example of a "Christian people" on the face of the earth, suddenly and for years becomes cruel, savage, uncontainable, organizes armed bands, makes forays over the countryside, lays ambushes, undergoes reprisals, lets off a store of age-old rage — and then returns to quiet and resignation.

This phenomenon, in European civilization, goes by the name of Peasant Resistance. It has taken place not only in Italy, but in France, Greece, Russia, Spain, and elsewhere. It is a phenomenon generally neglected by history, perhaps because history does not know how to handle it, and in any case finds it of little importance. But I have always been astonished by the fact that literature ignores it too: and yet it is a "romantic" (in the sense of "romance" or "narrative") phenomenon *par excellence,* since it is born of the passions and not of ideology.

In that explosion, whole worlds were born and died: loves, massacres, small communities, new forms of justice — even new currencies, each in its own tiny city-state. These worlds, like "drifting" continents, shifted and merged with others, and this may be the origin of the phenomenon itself, the contact between worlds (of men and women) that previously had no knowledge of each other: German Europeans, Mediterranean Europeans, soldiers, monks, peasants, homosexuals, middle-class Americans, bishops, popes, torturers . . . And, of course, animals, since each animal has its own world. Perhaps somewhere I ought to boast, I can't say with what degree of seriousness, that all four of the genealogies populating the universe are represented in my novels: mankind, animals, angels, and devils. Of these, the one that is perhaps missing in *Life Everlasting* is precisely the first: mankind. Because the history and stories here recounted are the object of neither consciousness nor memory — and this is not "proper" to mankind. This is what I hoped to achieve in writing *Life Everlasting*: to recover these things from oblivion. Assuming that a novel can do all that.

Ferdinando Camon

Padua, 1987

LIFE EVERLASTING

PART ONE

1. *God's signature*

The pope is in direct contact with God, and every night when he goes to bed while the Swiss servant tucks him in, and the reason she's Swiss is so they can't talk, he goes over his day in a low voice and asks questions for the next day and when he wakes up in the morning he finds God's letter under his pillow with all the answers and suggestions set down in writing and signed, when a pope dies he leaves the pile of spotlessly clean white letters to his successor but every so often a different-looking one turns up in the middle of the stack, one that with time has turned black because it's a false letter written by the devil and contains opposite instructions, ever since the devil started this trick of interfering in the correspondence between God and the pope things have become complicated because the pope hasn't always been able to pick out which of the two letters is the right one, at times he's made a mistake and that's meant calamities and wars and invasions. After the first world war the pope decided to look up the two letters found under his pillow on the night Italy intervened and have them examined by experts to see if there was any difference in the handwriting so that for the future as well he'd be able to distinguish the devil's hand and burn his message while paying strict attention to the divine one. Our village is convinced that the papal curia doesn't meet all at once but that the cardinals are summoned one at a time in order of importance, and this order changes depending on the subject under discussion, for the examination of the handwriting the first to come dancing in was the cardinal scribe who'd read God's messages many times and therefore confined himself to comparing the form of the letters and the kind of ink and the flourishes on the vowels and consonants without finding anything to object to and so with a bow he slunk over to one side, next the cardinal for foreign affairs came slinking in making a bow and carrying a large book under his arm in which all the most famous forgery cases that have taken place in the world were collected, but none of them resembled the devil's forgery, and so the cardinal went dancing over to the side, until finally they were all standing in groups along the walls whispering among themselves disconcerted and bewildered and moving from one group to another by pirouetting silently and devotedly in their cloth slippers, while the pope seated solitary and taciturn in the middle of the hall on his golden throne bowed his head and stroked his beard, when all of a sudden because of his fatigue or absentmindedness the two letters slip from his bony hands, the hands of an old man with stiff joints, and fall to the floor on the red carpet and the cleaning woman sees and picks them up and before handing them back she glances at them and letting out a cry makes the sign of the cross, what's the matter? ask the pope and cardinals in a single voice, there's a sin, answers the old woman pale and pointing to the devil's letter, where? where? they ask astounded, right there she says pointing with her finger to the signature on the false letter, the pope takes it in his hand and looks at it bringing it close to his myopic little eyes and squinting his eyelids and no sooner has he deciphered the first consonant than he becomes still paler and older and falls on his knees and so they pass the letter from one to another and as they slowly read it they become horrified and kneel down in expiation, the fact is that the devil's letter was written on the same white paper that looked like angel fluff and with the same ink and in the same handwriting as God's, only the signature was different because it began with a small letter: god. Naturally God would never have committed this lack of respect toward himself and on the other hand the devil couldn't allow that the name of his enemy be written with a capital letter and his not, so while the cleaning woman wafted the gentle flatulencies of Their Eminences out the window with an ostrich-plume fan, the trick was discovered that had time and again unleashed disasters on the world, and so for many years, that is to say a quarter of a century, people lived and worked in peace ensured by the pope who is the leader of humanity, and every morning punctually received only the letter with the proper recommendations which he promptly distributed to the four corners of the world.

No one in the village was ever told how that war ended, and anyway no one had the wish to look into it or ask questions. Seasons followed seasons and the years the years, the fogs came back every November descending in clouds and in the spaces between them the thrushes circled in flocks and migrating birds took a nosedive as soon as the mists parted and they saw the glistening vines and reddish leaves of the late-season vineyards. There were years so cold that pheasants came to sleep in the henhouses strutting forward with multicolored plumage while the vulgar hens got out of their way evacuating the more comfortable spaces and pecking their fleas to one side so as not to contaminate their guests, there were nights of such stiff frost that leaves froze to the core and if you touched them by mistake they crumbled like crackers, there were springs so windy that by lifting your nose you could smell the odor of petroleum from some ship moored in Venice or Trieste with its engines running.

Peace had continued for so many years it had come to seem eternal, and work had been progressing so well it appeared to have become a pastime or a game, something not to be interrupted even if it rained. Long rows of field hands, men and women, were to be seen on the open ridges, all identically dressed like scarecrows and therefore indistinguishable from one another, who sowed their seeds by scooping them up in handfuls from their aprons, or hoed together in a fish-spine pattern, or in the middle of the tobacco fields counted the leaves and decided that for that year eight of them should be left for each shoot, eight big leaves that provided it didn't storm opened profusely at right angles to the rays of the sun and swelled with warmth and dryness and later cut and threaded on a string were hung downwards in the huge drying sheds of Doralice and Castelbaldo where after a week the Treasury police came to count them one by one and take them away. The lucky man who entered a tobacco shop and came across a cigar made with our leaves would roll his eyes after the first puff rocking back and forth for all that pleasure, and going back in the store he'd buy out the whole stock of cigars and go away with the box under his arm. In the culvert, at the end of the tobacco fields, were basins full of yellow acid in which to immerse your arms and wait for the tobacco tar to dissolve, tar that makes the hairs on your arms and the backs of your hands stick together so when you wash with soap it feels as though they're being pulled with a pair of tweezers. The field hands worked from morning to night but it would be better to say from eight to eight because there were days so uniform and with the light so murky that to pass the time from morning to night was like going through a long tunnel pausing every so often to calculate how far you'd gone and how much farther you still had to go, looking from here at the little opening of light that looks like the gleam of a needle and from there at the gleam of light that looks like the eye of a needle, and when you're halfway you don't know any more or rather don't remember which glimmer of light is the entrance and which the exit, in this state of mind after the noontime break during which they ate Indian fashion with their legs crossed under their backsides and the kerchief that served as a tablecloth open in front of them where they spread a few hunks of bread and soup bones and hard-boiled eggs around a flask of wine, the field hands spontaneously, without agreeing in advance, dozed with their backs against the trunk of a poplar and now and then in their sleep took advantage of this position to scratch their backs by wriggling their shoulders a little with their hats smelling of sweat pulled down over their eyes, while the younger women who didn't feel the need to sleep combed each other's hair and deloused each other remarking with little bursts of laughter over the capture of the biggest vermin and squashing them between two fingernails to split them in two. There were weeks so idle that the only mishap worth talking about may have been furnished by Fatso who while slumbering swollen with wine on the edge of a ditch had leaned to one side at a certain point thus shifting the center of his bulk and had rolled softly, without making a splash, into the muddy water which by chilling his sweat had awakened him so suddenly that he opened his arms as though an inner spring had been released, but the cold feeling didn't bother him much and actually tempered the heat of the wine so that he preferred to finish his siesta where he was and not squander energy that anyway he didn't have. When they woke up from the siesta and looked around sluggishly someone would ask is it morning or afternoon? afternoon answered whoever had his wits about him, assuming there was one, and if there wasn't they were left in doubt and resumed their work until the whistle of the blackbirds, dropping like stones among the mulberries and calling to each other to reassemble their families, made it clear that night was approaching and therefore it was time to stop work and break up, each field hand starting for home with his hoe on his shoulder. All of a sudden on those days so gray and damp and devoid of sounds, or perhaps so full of sounds that you heard nothing, as though you were walking in a dream or on the bank of a rushing stream and even when striking the hard soil with the hoe to pulverize it you saw the clod of earth disintegrate in complete silence, all of a sudden someone lifted up his face and said it's raining, but another whose sensitivity lay in the palms of his hands, instead of on his inflamed face or in his eyes which looked like two fried eggs in a skillet, stretched out his hand focused his attention on his fingertips and said no, still it was as though it were raining because in fact the water came trickling down along the leaves of the trees and from there enveloped the branches and then the trunks where however the rough bark fractured it into countless tiny particles as fine as mist which you could see glistening without feeling it drip, until everyone was convinced it wasn't raining at all just when it was really starting to rain and the horizon disappeared in the haze as though evaporating and the plumes of smoke from the houses and huts twined around each other and creeping close to the ground imbued the vegetation with a smell of burning.

It was said that those people in Padua, a big city that has a saint with no name, a meadow with no grass, and a café with no doors, had brought the electric light as far as Este and were about to bring it to Montagnana, and that those in Verona, a big city that has an arena with no sand, a river with no banks, and a Can Grande, a Big Dog with no bark, had brought the electric light as far as Legnago, and that now the big shots from the big cities were driving in sleek automobiles along the roads once built by Napoleon and going back and forth as they pleased even at night, and that in fact because of all that illumination there was no difference any more between day and night, which meant that anyone who was fed up with the world could even do just the opposite of everyone else, sleep by day, wake up in the evening, read the newspapers as soon as they came out and behave accordingly, assuming a worried or sad or hopeful expression depending on the events reported in the press and then go around on his own until twelve o'clock, since whether it's noon or midnight is all the same, then eat supper in a restaurant in the center of town with a waiter who serves him by going back and forth to the kitchen and another who stands beside him smiling and approving with deep bows everything he does, meaning the dishes he orders and the way he eats them and the refinement with which he swallows each mouthful and the amount of wine he pours himself each time, that is two fingers exactly not a hair more, and the way he sips it so that none of it falls, and even the little red drop that does fall on the white tablecloth, he approves that too, kowtowing over and over again, this bootlicker stationed beside the rich night-roaming customer, and he reserves his deepest bow for when the satisfied customer goes away without looking at the bill and leaving on the table a wad of money so enormous as to say it's a pleasure to eat and still more to pay. From there the customer heads for the entrances of the big department stores where the red carpets are rolled out at night for those who don't care to mingle with the vulgar daytime crowd that dirties everything and steals stockings and haggles over prices, and there he and his friends since it's Christmas wait for the record to be played for them that says Venite adoremus, then they enter the paradise of merchandise, make the sign of the cross with their wallets in their hands and kneeling down worship it all, and then getting to their feet they pick out the crème de la crème. So now these powerful gentlemen are bringing the electric light to the borders of their provinces the better to be able to oversee them with binoculars from the towers of the city, a den of thieves, a nest of vultures, and overturning the natural order of things to the point of changing night into day they drive along the roads ablaze with light like falcons before the storm along the paths of thunderbolts.

There was no danger however that they'd bring the electric light to our village since it's an out-of-the-way place scattered and organized on its own and probably isn't even shown on maps, it's only some overconscientious bishop who discovers it every quarter of a century and so when he passes through Montagnana in his car driven by a chauffeur in livery he pushes on a little farther to pay us a short visit. The bishop is the highest authority in the city and according to old Rapacina the one in Padua lives over the cathedral in an apartment with glass walls, even those in the bathroom because he's such an honest person that he has nothing to hide and a good quarter of the city's population and especially its idle ladies are always there in the street or at the bar opposite sitting on cane-bottomed chairs and aiming their binoculars to see how the bishop spends his day, he's always studying, turning the pages rapidly because he reads very quickly and with his head bent he follows four lines at a time, but every so often he gets bored and his attention wandering a little he becomes aware that the city is watching him and although he's already blessed it at dawn with two fingers he imparts a special supplementary blessing. We know the pope is nothing but the bishop of Rome, a quite special city built on seven hills that are the seven sacraments and which has killed seven kings who are the seven capital sins. They say that in ancient times a Roman emperor who was a barbarian, otherwise he wouldn't have been emperor, defeated and annihilated all the enemy armies and scattered quicklime over the dead and dying on the battlefields so that nothing would be left, neither laments nor grass nor bones. His last battle was fought against a horde of Mongols or Tartars or Germans, or rather all of them together, that came flooding down along the roads from the north with their cavalry and with wagons drawn by peasants captured in the fields and along the rivers with long lines of boats tied to each other by ropes, and the first boat in each line pulled the whole train and was full of prisoners and peasant slaves who rowed while the others were loaded with warriors who gave orders and ate and slept. Well, the emperor got ready to receive the foe right in a valley where many roads converged and which lay between two large rivers, and he put his land forces on the water and his water forces with their boats and everything on land, and when the bold rampaging enemy, roaring to high heaven, arrived and began his great maneuvers, the emperor opened the sluices so that the water poured out into the countryside which became a lake while the river beds dried up and became roads, and the enemy found himself paralyzed, his cavalry in the water and his boats on the roads, and was massacred and annihilated with no survivors, and after the victory the emperor had the sluices closed again so that nature returned to what it had been before, rivers with rivers and roads with roads. And walking over the battlefield followed by his scribe the emperor dictated his memoirs for posterity, ending his discourse with an epigraph written with the blood of the vanquished, red on white marble, which was set in the middle of the carnage and said: The enemy army came down from the north—it will not go back; when along came the pope, dressed in white on his personal little donkey, followed by his cardinals holding a gilded umbrella over his head to protect him from the sun, taking his own sweet time like someone who has all eternity at his disposal, and steering his way between one corpse and another, he paused to decipher the stone squinting his myopic little eyes and shaking his head; to the emperor he said: And the men of your army came into the world—will they perhaps go back? And the emperor, already old and seized by despair, groped his way among his officers and the soldiers of his bodyguard calling them by name and touching them as though they were already dead and from time to time his own name too escaped his lips and he put his hands to his face and tore his hair. White hair.

2. *The Crua women*

Our battles in those years were fought against the inhabitants of the underground world, because when the rat population gets so large that it digs a network of tunnels under the houses of the village, the town hall sends a clerk with the register in his hand and his glasses on his nose and the map in his pocket, and he rides around on his bicycle checking to see if the houses are inhabitable and as he goes in, because his left foot is lame he loudly stamps his right one, shod with a wooden sole, and immediately hears the emptiness echoing underneath, and because his right ear is deaf with his left one he figures the size and length of the tunnel and draws it on the map and then makes you sign with an X and explains that within a week you should put sulphur. So Mamo, also called the Mouse because he had a face like one, whose house was smaller than the one dug by the rats under his floor, went out to get some sulphur and borrow a bellows and coming back stuck the nozzle of the instrument in the main tunnel and worked the handles to blow compressed sulphur through the underground passageways, which could be heard rumbling and swelling while the rats with wings opened themselves a hole and flew away to change their residence and their little ones tried hurriedly to grow up and have wings ahead of time, with the sole result that dead heaps of them were later found, big-bellied and limp, equipped with useless stumps and their mouths turned upward in their effort to reach the sky. It once even happened that the sulphur was applied with too much pressure, bursting the thin walls between all the underground tunnels so that they became connected and everybody heard the blind flight of the crazed bats passing under his own house fleeing the bitter and unbreathable wind puffed by the bellows, and so the peasants, frightened and worried, decided to put an end to it and exterminate the underground jungle by blasting it out for once and for all. Collecting all the bellows from the surrounding villages, except for Marega with which there are no diplomatic relations, they kept puffing away from so many different openings that the lighter one-story houses made of sun-dried brick rose on one side and collapsed on the other almost as though they were rocking on the waves the way the houses do in Venice, while in front of the tavern in the central square of the village the old people had assembled to receive bulletins with the news and results, and when they heard that a tunnel had opened at the Sleepers or Tre Lupie or Degora they sent boys rushing on bicycles with buckets of mortar on the handlebars to stop up the hole. By now a kind of spontaneous understanding among the various districts of the village had been set in motion and everybody felt ripe for mutual cooperation, they brought tools and ropes and shovels and spades, they mixed mortar nonstop, and distributed the tasks among themselves better than if they'd already carried out hundreds of drills, and when it was learned that the Crua house, more a hut than a house, had been flooded with sulphur and had caught fire, even before one of the Crua girls, screaming her misfortune all the way at the top of her lungs, had come teetering on a bicycle into the center of the village, an emergency squad had already left and arriving on the spot saved what could be saved. On examining the soil they were astonished that the house hadn't been built four yards to one side where the terrain was higher and more solid and provided both better drainage and better air, and with the further advantage that from there the facade looked south and you could eat outside facing the sun, and so the Crua women, who, poor things, have no man in the family, got back a more modern house than they had before and became a kind of symbol of village unity and were themselves felt to be common property, with the result that from that evening on more than one boy claimed the right to spend the whole night with them, since besides the Crua girls though rather unsociable from solitude, like wild animals pursued by hunger and fear, still weren't bad-looking and you could see that their bodies under their light little dresses were well shaped and all they needed was to put on a little weight with some hot polenta and grilled salami. They didn't look at all like old Mother Crua, who had a triangular face with nothing human about it, a soft nose like a fleshy sack, and little eyes and a mouth that were always closed like three orifices the size of pinheads, only her skull, huge as a pot and with hair like tow, seemed inhabited by a ghost of thought, lost in the inner bliss of a calm stupidity well disposed to death, and sitting by herself she gave no sign of hearing the words spoken around her and even when some rude boy as an experiment shouted in her ear she didn't budge; in fact she didn't have ears, just two tiny branches red as coral, mere vegetal excrescences, which every morning the youngest daughter cleaned with a little feather brush with the same loving care with which you'd dust a precious knick-knack that you wouldn't want to break. The little Crua girl was the meekest and most resigned of the sisters, it was as though the fact that she didn't mind being always treated as the lowest was written on her forehead.

One day when all the underground animals devastated by sulphur were banging against both sides of the dark tunnel walls and bumping into each other, squeaking and biting with their beaks or open mouths, while through the whole village rumbled a sound like a herd of buffaloes let loose at a gallop since the hollow underground spaces multiplied the echo, which is why in winter the children like to go to school with hobnails on their wooden soles because they can slide on the ice in the ditches and during these sprints it's fun to hear the ice, which buckles as it forms leaving an air space above the water, go boom (a boy named Cargalletto fell through the ice into the warmish water to re-emerge two yards farther on; we could see his frightened eyes and his palms beating against the pane of ice, while the dog that accompanied him to school started yelping to call for help), on that day Mamo had gone running to the little Crua girl to show her the underground world, tearing her away from her new hut with its zinc roof, and while she persisted in giving a final cleaning with the feather brush to the coral ears of her mother, who kept her head bowed for this, he had dragged her outside whining but submissive and carried her off to the river, the big artery through which all the blood of the village runs. Under the hillock where Mamo, all spruced up and exhilarated, and the tearful little Crua girl sat opened an underground cavern that lost itself in countless ramifications connected by winding tunnels, and animals dislodged from their nests by the odor of Hell, and thrown into flight like soldiers without masks before the onslaught of gas, burst out of it, shoving and clawing each other in a blind sharing of life or death, and on that hillock for the whole evening and the early hours of the night the boy and girl amused themselves by checking the results of this mortal struggle and betting who would be first to spot another survivor bursting out toward life, and as night fell the animals took on strange and unknown shapes, enlarged by a veil of tears or joy, indescribable shapes in the imagination of the Crua girl, who for the first time in her life felt her brain melt and spin dizzily with brand new gears like those of a baby, so that at a certain point she stopped betting with her friend who in fact now seemed to her a little naive and lacking in something and unsound. A flying ant, he said, getting to his feet and pointing his finger at a black butterfly with black wings and black head and black eyes that was fluttering zigzag as though drunk with air along a beam of moonlight. A mouse with wings, said the Mouse, pointing to a pony prancing in the air and ascending in a spiral with long contented neighs, and when it turned in her direction it may have paused a little and stared at her with the saddest human eyes, it can happen that a person through no fault of his own finds himself trapped in the body of a horse and then decides not to rebel and to behave like a horse but you can see from the eyes that he's thinking of his misfortune and when he looks at you he gives you the shivers like those now going up and down the Crua girl's spine. Look there goes a marten, said the Mouse, jumping to his feet as though frightened by the appearance of a land-and-water, water-and-land animal, a delightful creature long and slender but not broad, which means it can work its way between one thing and another and dodge them both, it's able to pass between two adjacent blades of grass without uprooting them, and when it runs it's all feet under a body and when it swims it's all oars under a boat, it doesn't have many thoughts, but always just one at a time, and when it's fleeing death by sulphur this single thought is fear as you can see in its eyes, when it's safe and sound this single thought is rage as you can see by its little white teeth which it shows by drawing its lips back in a snarl, and when it's arrived on the other side the animal no longer has even one thought or even one memory and you can tell from its ugly snicker that it's freed itself from everything and that if a female of its own kind were to turn up it would immediately make her pregnant without a thought for its mate that had just died. Now the Mouse had figured out the direction of the underground passage in the stretch leading to the outlet, and shuttling back and forth between the river and the bank he shifted position some twenty yards back, then putting his ear to the ground started guessing what kind of animal was coming out next. A furious whistling buzz indicated a family of winged ants, a constant bumping sound against the roof of the tunnel indicated bats stubbornly intent on reaching the sky like butterflies under glass, while four-footed animals came with a frantic patter of little footsteps, and since all they had at their disposal was the space of the floor they rammed and straddled and bit each other, their progress interrupted by somersaults and brawls and actual battles among whole flocks of them in total darkness. As soon as they emerged from the hole the aquatic animals rolled instinctively into the water like falling stones, the land animals immediately turned right or left, and the winged ones continued the thrust of their flight for another few yards and then rose delightfully into the sky as though sucked up by the moon. For by now it was night and it was as dark outside as in the bowels of the earth, with the difference that outside the darkness was blue while inside it was black, but in that blue flooded with white the colors stood out better, and the little Crua girl, her mouth open and watering, now realized with wonder that the underground world is full of colors or rather since it has so little light its colors are brighter in return. A horse has dropped down on the rippling water of the river and drinks in long draughts that sound like the shrill chirping of crickets, then the rider twitches the reins and the horse jerks its head up, its circular little eye gleams in the moonlight and it's obvious from that gleam that the animal is strong, and while the rider gives a condescending wave of his hand and the girl responds by bowing her head while following the scene out of the corner of her eye, the horse breaks into a gallop so swift it can't even be heard and since it doesn't touch the grass it could actually be flying if it weren't that the movements of its four legs cleaving the air are precisely those of a gallop, and indeed the cow with the moon stuck on her horns, grazing lazily with outspread legs and dangling udder and every so often raising her stupid eye, whether to make some observation about the world around her or about the grass she'd swallowed and was digesting inside her wasn't clear, that broad heavy cow standing there as though planted on the ground or rather sunk in it up to the level of her teats would never have been capable of flying, not that the Crua girl had ever so much as dreamed that a cow could fly, but a horse yes, not so much because it's light and swift as because it always holds its head high with an air of mystery as though it found itself on this earth by chance or by mistake. The most wonderful thing was how quickly the animals just born from the bowels of the earth decided then and there whether to be aquatic or earthbound or airborne or more than one at the same time, though some of them just stayed there with their muzzles in the air as though a little stunned by themselves and all these new things, and scurrying between the feet and lap of the Crua girl sitting on the hillock they quietly pondered, their muzzles to the ground, the advantages of having legs or fins or wings, or legs and wings, or fins and wings, or legs and fins, and before making their choice there by the dark hole they were all as shapeless as wandering shadows and with no great differences between them, but as soon as the choice was made, while each was setting out toward its own element, the great transformations began which the Crua girl by identifying with them noticed in her own body. The wild rabbit had an awkward and ineffectual gait and would always have liked to be a dove, and here it was lengthening its fleshy mouth and scratching it with its front paw or rather by now its white wing, feeling its bony beak and ruffling its feathers and circling around on its first flights while avoiding the river for fear of falling in; and the sulky mole, which had been burrowing in dead-end tunnels all its life, changing its mind in the darkness and turning back and then getting up its courage and going forward again so that by the end of the day it no longer knew which way was forward and which back, had dreamed of being able to fare forth on two fleshy wings to examine everything once and for all and possess the world by knowing it, and now here it had become a bat with only a slight transformation since it kept the same snout as before and the same velvet belly and was capering awkwardly on its hind legs and falling over on its back, since it wasn't able to guess what muscles to use in stretching its wings, and whimpering furiously walking up and down the legs of the Crua girl who kept giggling and squirming because it tickled; the marsh hen which though a bird liked only the reeds in rivers and all its life had had to perch on a vertical bamboo stalk with one leg folded up and one extended down, seeing nothing but its own image reflected in the water a couple of feet below and afraid of the boats that drifted with the current and looked empty or held a few cardboard boxes covered by a green net and all of a sudden there's a hunter inside who kills it and by the time it tumbles from leaf to leaf and hits the water the setter is right there waiting with shrewd eye and open jaws, the marsh hen had always hoped to be free of its love of water, to gain confidence with distance and spend foggy nights somewhat farther away from the river banks where waves of fog swirl in even the most sheltered holes, and now here it is extending its legs like a wading bird and beating the stumps of its wings to flee pell-mell across the open plains. All this the girl saw emerge from her lap to occupy the world, earth air and water, and then turn back toward its origin, indeed all the various kinds of little animals were swarming around as though to welcome her and climbing over her body and the ants with their big transparent wings got tangled in her hair and she heard their gay and festive buzzing as a greeting; she felt as though she were a broody hen sitting nicely with lowered head even when the newborn chicks push their way from under her wings, and since they're unable to see the world from inside the nest they climb up the mother's body to her back, slipping down again with great astonishment since they don't know the force of gravity, then starting all over again and frolicking to enjoy their own weight, till the first thing they see up there is the mother's comb and they go in single file along her neck to examine it with their eyes and peck it repeatedly to make sure what it is, and when the first one falls off the second moves forward and so on all day long without the hen budging an inch lost as she is in the bliss that comes from being starved for weeks on end and the suspicion that these new lives have come forth from her warmth and endurance. The rider too had returned on the horse with the swift hooves or swift wings, the animal with head lowered was drinking from the river in long draughts that like the shrill chirping of crickets could be distinctly heard, every so often the horse jerked its head up and its circular little eye gleamed in the moonlight and it was obvious from that gleam that the animal was strong, and while the rider gave a condescending wave of his hand the girl responded by bowing her head and lowering her eyes and instinctively looking at her lap, so it was all quite natural when the man came near her or rather was on top of her and as she yielded she reclined her head to one side on the grass and half closed her eyes because certainly there was no need to look him in the face, afterwards there was no need to do anything except wait for the most beautiful little animals in the world, which only she appreciated and understood, to emerge all over again from her lap, and it was she who'd help them decide what element to live in and what form to assume, fish or hare or bat, he was very handsome and strong and silent except for the deep breathing she could hear inside her ear where he was transferring his whole soul and when he gently moved away and jumped back on his horse, which broke into a gallop so swift it couldn't even be heard and since it didn't touch the grass it could actually have been flying if it weren't that the movements of its four legs cleaving the air were precisely those of a gallop, she sat up and rearranged her clothes and looked with a kind of pity at the Mouse who was still standing there like a fool. Awkwardly he gave her his hand and pulled her up, and without saying a word walked her back across the fields to her new house with the zinc roof, where Mother Crua was waiting for her in silence with her head bent and her ears like little branches of coral, which the girl seizing the feather brush began to clean, smiling softly to herself and every so often looking at her lap.

PART TWO

1. *The she-man*

Our people are born to live and die outside history, with days slipping by smoothly from morning to evening, with nights identical from evening to morning, because when there's nothing on which to take their bearings our folks get along perfectly well but when they're forced to focus on something it obstructs their vision. One summer noon so broiling hot it made the stones split, the Sette family, who manage very well by themselves in the middle of a sea of mud, saw a stranger wearing boots enter their yard; after hurrying to close and bolt the doors and windows they peeped out the cracks in the shutters for he really seemed intent on entering, and having kicked the door he walked all around the outside of the house muttering and hawking phlegm, and peeped in through the cracks himself, till Sette Secondo, the head of the family, and the stranger found themselves staring balefully at each other eye to eye through the same crack, and he went away. The family sat down at the table worried because that fellow could have been up to no good, and the children sat there stupidly with open mouths, gulping down their food without chewing it and getting it all over themselves. Next day at the tavern the head of the Sette family heard that a stranger passing through had asked where does my son Secondo live? and realized that the visitor was none other than his father

Sette Primo, and pleased as could be he went home and gave his children a slap on the back of the neck and told them the news: Guess who was here yesterday, kids, your grandpa! They were all excited by the idea that finally they'd seen their grandfather again after so many years of not knowing whether he was dead or alive, and all night long they didn't get a wink of sleep but kept turning back and forth in the big bed asking each other what did grandpa look like? and someone who had seen his eye described his eye, and someone who had seen his nose described his nose, and the rest of him they happily completed with the help of their imaginations.

Sette Secondo was a veteran of the world war, and later I'll tell you in his own words how he returned home from Caporetto, but much as he was convinced that that war had never ended, except by make-believe, but was still smoldering under the ashes and that you had to be on the alert and expect the Germans from one hour to the next, the fact is that when at a certain point the war broke out all over again, it caught us all by surprise and first of all Sette Secondo, who was a specialist in arrested development and kept seeing things when they weren't there anymore. One morning he comes home from the fields, dragging his feet from fatigue as though he had bricks on his shoes instead of soles, and three men all dressed alike come in from the road, I mean from the side where it's so clear a road is needed that among ourselves we pretend it's there, and one of the three is so fat his buttons are popping and Sette Secondo throws his arms around the man's middle saying cheerfully what a tub of lard, whereupon the man explodes like a bomb, gives him a bite on the neck, and throws him to the ground, and sticking his pistol in his mouth and bending over as much as his belly allows, he stands with teeth bared above his ear and yells and spits in it with such rage that you can't understand a thing except that he's mad. Meanwhile the second man stands at attention alongside the third, who's as blond and slender as a stalk of hemp with clothes as tight as an actress's and a face as thin and sharp as a knife, and it looks as though he doesn't even hear this ruckus and that the scene has nothing to do with him, in fact the only thing that concerns him to the point of exasperation is a blond curl that's slipped out from under his visor cap and which he can't seem to keep in place. The Hemp Stalk notices it by stooping limply over a puddle of water and looking at his reflection, and he goes on patting his face here and there, the expression of his mouth and eyes so full of boredom that it's obvious it won't be long before the boredom becomes something else. If he were a woman it would certainly become tears and if he were a man it would certainly become rage, but seeing as how he's himself it will become neither tears nor rage but rather a new form, and no one can say what it will be because no one can say what he is. The Hemp Stalk slowly straightens up and gazes around with bright metallic little eyes that look as though they're set perpendicular to the thin face like a hilt with respect to the dagger, and when his gaze lights on Sette Secondo it's as though he were planting that dagger in him, sharp as a pin and painful as it penetrates, until Sette Secondo almost had the feeling he'd been pierced all the way through, but when he looked more closely at the Hemp Stalk's face he saw that his gaze seemed out of focus and intent on something further behind Sette Secondo, and slowly turning around he saw that that something was his son Sette Sesto who had been bold enough to open the door of the house and stand there in full view, while his mother and brothers and sisters peered unseen through the cracks in the blinds and covered their dry mouths with their handkerchiefs. It must have been a rare occurrence for the Hemp Stalk to look at something with interest, and then whoever was close by felt obliged to pick the thing up and bring it to him; it must have been even rarer for the Hemp Stalk to look at someone with insistence, and then whoever was close by felt obliged to pick up that someone and bring him to him like an object; but this must have been the first time that the Hemp Stalk in his turn was being looked at with insistence by someone, and the surrounding air seemed to tremble and you could see that the Hemp Stalk's two attendants wanted somehow to erase such a scandal and cause the disappearance of that someone, for whom it would have been better had he never been born. When the scene was over the Hemp Stalk leaned his head to one side with the sad and tortured smile of the profaned god who discharges his pity on the world along with his revenge, while Sette Secondo at the Hemp Stalk's feet felt this compassion come over him, and it was so much and so heavy that as they carried away his son Sette Sesto, lifting him up with a stick under the armpits and hoisting him onto a jeep full of people that nobody had noticed, he was unable to shake off the load and get to his feet, while all the windows of the house were suddenly flung open and the women and children leaning out in clusters let out a wail such as was never heard at any funeral. Were he to live a thousand years, Sette Secondo would go on remembering every detail of that encounter, and even today every so often he pricks up his ears hearing the engine of a jeep starting up at the gate, but when he goes and looks he finds the gateway empty. His son was seen half an hour later for the last time at Urbana, one of a group of detainees who'd been unloaded from trucks and were being guarded by a platoon of Germans under the command of a big red angry one, with an outsize head like that of a cow, and all were awaiting orders. And now the jeep arrived, so silent it seemed to be coasting with its engine off, and in it were three Germans, two of whom jumped out as though catapulted by a spring, while the third still sat there engrossed, his head bent slightly forward and one delicate hand stroking his forehead in such a slight and meticulous motion that had he been a woman you might have said he was reshaping the line of his eyebrows from memory, but since he was a man you could only suspect he was suffering from a bad headache and was unable to dispel the knot of pain inside his skull. With much distress and by fits and starts, as though the vertebrae of his neck were stiff, he finally succeeded in lifting his head slightly and opening his rosy and transparent eyelids, as though they were a lowered stage curtain behind which the lights have been lit so that the actors can take their places and the scene be set before the curtain rises; the lights were his sick eyes, which seemed not to tolerate daylight, and the actors were his thoughts, which had now composed and arranged themselves to enact a scene that all the Germans present must by now have learned by heart. No sooner had the man passed his hands over his chest and stood up as though to get out of the jeep than a jolt ran through the soldiers that was quickly translated into increased vigilance and ferocity, but just as actors who for a fraction of a second when the curtain goes up allow themselves to cast a glance at the audience, so the eyes of the German commander seemed to mirror the group of prisoners standing motionless as though to have their picture taken, and next they seemed to undergo a little flicker of surprise at seeing their shirts and long underwear and bare feet, and then they seemed to see nothing more, as though instead of looking at the group in front of them his eyes were looking instead at the images of the group reflected within them. With the absent air of a sleepwalker the commander extended his slender feet from the jeep and with a little hop landed on the ground, where his immediate concern was to readjust the uniform delineating a slim and weak little body, sick, almost sick, young, very young, the body of an adolescent when the male has barely begun to differentiate himself from woman. It was apparent at once that this commander was very much alone because there was no one to keep him company or if there was that person certainly wasn't there, for he didn't seem to see anyone, either Italian or German, but only himself, moving not as in the world but in the midst of his own thoughts, which were keeping him sad company. He walked along in front of the group as if it didn't exist, and at a certain point he must have found himself faced with a new and unforeseen thought, for he stopped, brought his ankles together, and standing with his hands behind his back slowly drew himself up and focused his gaze, his chin making a kind of upward jerk, almost as though the boy commander were feeling a sudden fury because of his pain, and acting upon an unsuspected energy had decided to pay it no mind but to do what had to be done, thoroughly and without qualms. Standing erect, he turned on his heels to the left and strode swiftly to the jeep, where he hopped back in and reseated himself, looking proudly with folded arms into the faces of that group of frightened tatterdemalions who seemed to huddle together, and after a minute of this cutting stare from his dagger-shaped face it was as though his inner energy had all of a sudden deserted him, and as his gaze flagged he withdrew from the world and lowering his brow began concentrating on a point within himself. The curtain had fallen, the drama was over, and the ess ess loaded the prisoners on the truck, shoving them by the shoulders and quick to separate any two who exchanged a few words, innocent as two sheep that hear each other chewing just when they've both pulled up the same clump of grass and without disputing swallow it, one from one end and one from the other, each savoring exactly half, and then satisfied with this justice rub muzzles in a mutual exchange of thanks. The truck departed and shortly thereafter so did the silent jeep, with the Hemp Stalk leaning back in the seat as though to relax, and as he went by in profile before the onlookers it seemed to some that his lips had a kind of smirking smile.

That day the Hemp Stalk visited each district of all the local villages, and wherever he went he left a mark like the lash of a whip. However much death may disfigure and gut and rot a body, when the moment comes in the hereafter, and it will come very soon because God Almighty's patience has reached its limit, among all those millions and millions of peoples it won't take but a glance to find his skull, shaped like a dagger of bone, to place ourselves half on his right and half on his left, and escort him en masse as witnesses for the Last Judgment, and we want to see whether he'll decide to open his mouth or not when the avenging angels extract his tendons to make strings for their violins.

That evening neither Sette Sesto's brothers nor those of the other men who'd been rounded up returned to their families, and it looked as though their houses were uninhabited and dead, invaded and occupied by silence. During the days that followed in one family after another a boy would suddenly be missing who later from time to time sent news of himself in the most unexpected ways: a beggar, for instance, as he was being given a flask of wine or a portion of polenta in charity would pull a note out of his socks and without looking hand it over, or a kid on his way to school would stick his little weasel face in the window and say, as if he knew all about it, Lightning's doing all right. For now that they'd gathered in the Swamp and formed bands armed with machine guns brought by the Russian and English prisoners escaping from the San Fidenzio camp, and organized themselves into patrols of eleven or twelve men (never more than fourteen, never less than ten), the boys had changed their names and rechristened themselves Lightning, who'd been Frison, Lizard, Soso, Kira, who'd been poor Biscazzo and was later to pay the price for everybody, Quicksand, but that had always been his nickname, Katia, who all the same was a man, Ken, Ischia, Boots, Xerxes, Tarzan, and so forth. Of all these, the best of our kind, which has always produced only hairy-assed apes, not one is left, and the only reminder is some jam container filled with earth and with a dried-up flower in the middle deposited where the disaster took place, at one end of a bridge or the side of a road or in the woods of the Swamp, but all of them are up there with heads bowed waiting for the violin concert to start so they can say politely, excuse us, dear angels, but the strings of your violins aren't quite tight enough, and thus get the angels to stretch them even to the breaking point. I was one of the last to leave for the Swamp. At Castelbaldo a partisan action group had emerged that soon fell apart, having been commanded by a traveling salesman who was struck down while on his way to visit his girl friend, the girl friend lived far away and he had to take too many roads which meant he was always as dusty as a miller (the report is still obscure), and by another salesman who was found dead and it's not known how he died since he was always alone and no one knew his name.

The English had brought a radio with them and in the middle of the woods had set up an antenna as tall as a lightning rod, and from there every evening they were able to hear their own language. It was as though they were the masters and we the guests, since they were informed of the operations to be carried out and the necessary moves, and finally one night they heard the message from London saying the rain has stopped. This was the advance notice, and the order for the night parachute drop was the wind is calm. A squad led by Tempesta set out, and anyone meeting it had to know the password black panther. The men were stationed in pairs at the four corners of a large bumpy stretch of grassy terrain, in the middle of which a red signal light was placed pointing upward with its lamp operated by hand, two quick flashes and a long one, two quick flashes and a long one, like that, get it wrong and you're in trouble. The airplane began to descend till it was almost touching the trees, making such a roar it seemed to be accompanied by celestial organs with their pipes stretching all the way to the moon, the seraphim were singing and we without realizing it were singing along with them. After three passes it flew the length of the field and lit two white tail lights, then extinguished them, and we were afraid we were being left behind in the midst of the krauts. Then two green lights and a red one, then three red lights, and now it looked just like the cross of Jesus Christ with drops of blood at the three long ends, and seeing it each of us was convinced that these were friends. The wish came to open our arms and wave our hands, and in the dim light amid the roar from the powerful engines of the plane, which had dropped to two hundred meters over our heads, each of us had the impression that his comrades in front of him were also stretching out their arms. On the fourth pass it made a drop, on the fifth, sixth, and seventh pass it flew the length of the field and made drops. In all there must have been thirty-six parachutes, nine at a time. The plane left, the cross returned to its heaven, and the pipe-organ symphony was over, but the parachutes were seen falling into the Fratta river and the swamps. The men went rushing from the field toward the footbridge, which was being guarded by Tempesta, he asked for the password, and instead of answering the men laughed and laughing they died, still astonished as Tempesta mowed them all down in a burst of gunfire. It was a tragic mistake and I'm sure that by now these poor dead men will have understood that they shouldn't have laughed, and if they haven't understood, it won't be hard to explain it to them when we have time. Here I can only say that Tempesta's not to blame for the loss of their lives, nor even for leaving the corpses there to gasp out their last breath half submerged in the water, because the important thing was to recover at least part of the materiel. Setting to work in boats we retrieved about ten boxes, but one contained only ammunition and dynamite, no weapons, and the others were full of cigarettes, binoculars, canned salmon and anchovies, butter, tea, coffee, and sugar, all worse than useless. We carried the stuff back to our hideout in the Swamp, and next day gazing with the binoculars from the tops of the tallest trees we saw the Germans arrive with their trucks on the banks of the river, where they inflated some rubber rafts and rowed off in all directions through the marshes, to return with many boxes, which they lined up and opened and took away with them. There were automatic rifles and hand grenades and several machine guns and even a small cannon, and afterwards we saw them taking pictures of the dead, first lying down and then being held upright from behind by the jacket or hair; we immediately figured they'd go from house to house showing these photographs to the women and children in order to discover the families of the dead and massacre them on the threshing floor. For the same reason one of the dead men was put in a life jacket and lowered into the river with a rope around his neck tied to a pole, and on the pole was a sign and on the sign his name, since his name had been found but not his village and so the only way to find out where he came from was to make his fellow villagers rush en masse to the river banks with the wish to pull the drowned man out.

Our leader in the Swamp was that fellow Remo who today is suspected of treason. Remo was not from one of our villages and he claimed to be an officer. He had a round face that looked as though it had been measured with a compass, a curved nose situated not under but between his eyes, and two big round eyes that took up his whole forehead, thus there was no space left for the forehead and eyebrows, and in fact his eyebrows instead of being above his eyes went around them, with even a few little hairs continuing underneath, and since he was bald but with a little goatee you always had the disagreeable sensation in looking at him that his head had been cut off by mistake and then stuck back on before the blood had had a chance to dry but in the hurry and confusion had been put upside down with the eyes over the brows and the hair on the chin. With his brain pan reduced to a minimum Remo was incapable of thought, and at most subject throughout his whole body to emotional tremors that seemed like pure animal sensitivity. Whenever he stood still he always put his weight on his left leg, while continually bending his right knee back and forth, his hands behind his back, and he'd curl his tongue between his open lips, expelling air as from a punctured tire. With that owl face of his, the minute you stared at him he showed a flash of irritation at your curiosity and shooting up his eyebrows in such a way that they completely surrounded his eyes he stared back at you, tilting his head to one side just like an owl. He had this advantage over us, that with a face like that he discouraged any discussion and even any questions. When questions were put to him he batted his eyebrows more quickly than ever and then suddenly stopped, keeping them lowered like an owl captured by day and forcibly held in one's hands to face the sun. If after this point you asked one more question, he walked away and disappeared, leaving behind as a souvenir and explanation a gob of saliva dangling between two stalks of couch grass, just as the owl with a flap of its wings slips out of your hands, and its intestines wrung by the exertion, squirts between your fingers a little deposit of warm shit.

2. *Provisional life*

Sette Secondo never did understand who his enemies were in the war, Germans or Austrians or Croats or Italians, as far as he was concerned he didn't trust any of them, neither those in the trenches in front of him nor those alongside or behind him. Besides one of his comrades was a Sicilian, who was himself so distrustful that he always slept with a knife under his head so as to be able to defend himself against anyone at all. The Sicilian was unable to speak because as a child he'd never learned to move his mouth properly but always kept it wide open and with a flushed look as though he were having a perpetual orgasm, and no sooner did they leave him in peace in the trench or barracks than he really fell to having an orgasm whether other people were there or not and as though he were alone in the world. The sound emitted by his vocal cords came out disguised through his crooked nasal passages, and this was all to his advantage because since nobody could understand him, he took the liberty of never saying yessir and nossir, but endlessly argued about every order he was given, varying the sounds as though he were improvising an organ concert on the spot. The worst was when they distributed the grappa rations in the trenches, then the man protested with gestures as well, and yelled and shook his head and walked back and forth through the trench muttering at everybody and especially anyone he caught in the act of drinking. Apparently he insulted them so much that his comrades came to understood the man's mistake, assuming he was a man because it should be noted that half an hour after mess he was still chewing his cud as though he'd regurgitated it from his stomach, and when he had to do his business he didn't squat but simply bent over and discharged a volley of hard green pellets like a goat, the man's mistake was in believing that the grappa was a kind of reward paid in advance by the bosses for going over the top, which meant that if they all got together and agreed not to drink, no one would have the right to order the company to go on the offensive since the company hadn't accepted the conditions, and there weren't any acceptable conditions because it wasn't a normal sort of job. He didn't go along with it and didn't understand why he was there, and when he'd been called up and they'd distributed two sheets to him and a uniform, he'd been trapped forever by accepting this stuff, unfamiliar stuff since he had to ask for a practical demonstration on the use of sheets, and now one had to wait for the contract to expire. It expired at Caporetto and the whole army went away whistling softly and without weapons, except for a few groups of peasants who by touching the soil with their feet and picking it up in their hands and crumbling it between their fingers and tasting it like powder on their tongues, checked its chemical composition and quality and decided it wasn't worth the trouble to leave. To convince themselves thoroughly they hoed a square yard of soil with their bayonets and then two or three of them pissed on it and calculated without a watch the time it took for it to soak in, and each made a comparison with the rate of absorption of the red soil of Vicenza, the black soil of Pavia, the rich soil of Foggia, the soft soil of Mantua, the hard soil of Sassari. They stood there on that no-man's land, and those who had no home threw away their uniforms and went back to being peasants, and taking possession of the first demolished house they found they reappeared on the threshold with a spade in their hands to wait peacefully for the Germans, while those who had families stood with legs spread gazing in dismay at their broken-down shoes from which the wet end of their puttees stuck out, and then disgruntled they left, shaking their heads with the cheated look of someone who faced with the choice between two available sisters has just married the ugly one. And to think that for all those years they'd managed to hold out in the trenches, which are like ditches without water and serve as both kitchen and latrine. But cooking was almost never followed by eating. Once the food was heated up and laid out nicely on a flat stone that served as a table in front of your knees, and if you've heated it properly with lumps of solid naphtha which burns with a rarefied blue flame like the breath of a mule, and all you have to do is put a leaf in front of it so the enemy can't see it, and the soup gives off an appetizing aroma that almost succeeds in overcoming the stench of the excrements scattered around in the trench, then no sooner have you curled up in your well-sheltered hole where not even stray bullets can find you and before you even have time to swallow your first mouthful, already there's the usual Croat, with his broad flat face like a shovel, standing over your trench against the sky and snatching your food with a greedy hand, and if you're not quick enough to grab his legs and pull him down he slips away like a ghost, and then you can hear him munching your grub in his burrow ten yards away. The reason they're called Croats is because they like their food crude, they go crazy over raw pumpkin with a side dish of raw potatoes. If on the other hand you're on the lookout for the Croat and while chewing keep your eyes on the sky, then your rations get lifted by your buddy on the right, who's an enemy too, and when you put your hand on the stone you're using as a table you find that someone else's tongue has already licked up even the crumbs. This is what the Italian or Slav peasants were doing, while the Germans being a warlike race were always so good at going without eating that by now their heads were dancing around in their ever more outsize helmets and the circles under their eyes looked suffused by a blood that had turned to water, as happens to consumptives. They'd go into action after these miserable daily brawls over a ladleful of beans were over, and as night fell they'd begin disturbing the sleep of the bersaglieri by crowing cock-a-doodle-doo in chorus, because the bersaglieri wear feathers on their heads like the backsides of roosters but don't like to hear about it; until midnight you'd think you were in a silly chicken house unable to take advantage of what little time there is for rest or to imagine that the housewife will shortly fling open the door and drive all these fluttering lice-ridden fowls out into the daylight with her broom. Then all of a sudden the Germans stop disturbing the Italians' slumber, wait half an hour or so for them to go fast asleep, and then split up into small patrols with tow tied around their feet so as not to make noise, and crawling on all fours like hyenas, nature having already given them the faces of hyenas, they move forward along our communication trenches their bayonets clamped in their teeth and cut the throats of the sleeping men who, yes, immediately scream but the scream no longer finds the windpipe which has been cut and so it comes out in the form of a sigh, spattering around the dugout a sick bad blood by now fed up with flowing. Next morning the captain would count the corpses and always ended up rather disappointed that there were still so many mouths to feed, and yet after all these years there were now very few, so it was clear that the captain's secret ideal was to wake up happily and calmly one fine dawn and looking around find himself alone, safe and sound in his dugout, the most secure and best equipped one since it even had a straw-bottomed stool with a hole in the seat for his bodily needs, and there with his hands folded on his belly to keep gazing left till the mule appeared loaded with cooked savoy cabbage and hardtack and once everything was unloaded to start gulping it down without a care in the world, stuffing his flabby gut down to its smallest interstices, and then to sink still deeper into his tomb and from there with upturned face to observe the rounds of shrapnel and artillery shells and cannon passing over in different directions and the echoing fusillades from the infantry patrols, and once he had the whole picture to figure out the movement of units: Serbs on the right, Croats straight ahead, our boys holding fast! Next day, a rotation of forces: Croats on the right, Serbs straight ahead, our boys holding fast! And the third day, the most awful situation in all its details: Serbs and Croats on the right, Germans straight ahead, all of them victorious, and our boys no more! Wiped out by the artillery, smashed and blown to bits, making it necessary to ask for a truce and meticulously begin the job of collecting and reassembling the corpses. First whichever corpses were intact or almost so were laid out next to each other, because if all that was missing was an eye or finger or hand you couldn't very well waste time looking for it in all those trenches and foxholes, and anyway for all you knew that soldier might always have been cockeyed or with a stump, but the search was worth the trouble if the missing part was the head, though when all was said and done the space once occupied by the missing skull could be covered with the helmet by fastening the buckle to the collar of the jacket, and even more so if the part blown off was an arm or a leg or half the body, in that case the search got frantic and it usually happened that the arm missing from the disemboweled corpse under a tree had got caught for some reason up in the branches, and this was a sure sign that he'd been a lookout ordered up there as punishment since he was a Milanese hooligan who liked to give people a hard time, and even there in the tree with the binoculars he had put his whole felon's store of energy and courage into the task of frustrating the sniper. Once the corpses had been gathered up a superior officer came to check the operation, and raising his hand to his helmet he saluted the dead with the irritated gaze with which a city dweller watches a flock of sheep being driven past his windows and dirtying the streets, but in the end his gaze became furious and his face purple and he was seized by an undignified frenzy because every time he discovered an incomplete corpse it was always that of some officer, while for their comrades in the unit the soldiers always succeeded in reassembling a whole body, even at the cost of attaching two left legs or two right arms to the trunk. There had even been the time when so as not to send away in such a mutilated state a corporal who'd been cut in half by shrapnel, sliced through at the height of the navel to be exact, since a thorough search hadn't turned up the other half and now the truce was about to end and the men in white overalls from the Red Cross standing there with cans of quicklime to scatter over the irretrievable corpses were stewing with impatience, and since they suddenly found another half of a corporal, he too sliced at the navel, they joined the two of them, forming a sort of king of spades. When the superior officer surveyed the bodies thus reassembled a sort of unusual interest appeared in his distracted gaze when confronted by this monster with two heads and four arms, and he stopped to look at it with his hand still to his helmet and that smirking military smile that so closely resembles a sneer, until slowly the corners of his mouth trembled as though the mockery that always stuck to them like a dead cigarette butt was about to fall and finally his whole mouth and jaws became distended and started gasping as though from a nervous spasm, and he burst out laughing uncontrollably. He let himself drop on the nearest stone and went on gasping and muttering, just-what-we-needed, just-what-we-needed, and raising his helmet he passed a handkerchief over his white hair to dry it for in his seizure he was sweating profusely. A red rocket burst in the air, giving the signal that the truce was over, whereupon two male nurses, one on each side, picked him up by the armpits and quickly dragged him away in this huddled position over the bare scorched plateau, and amid the whine of the first hail of bullets threw him down in the nearest dugout where he went on writhing with laughter and squealing like a crazed gorilla. This was the same colonel who came to check the practical results in the field of the new weapons and devices developed by the Department of Discoveries and Inventions, a department into which the most highly recommended candidates holding an elementary-school certificate and who weren't peasants had wormed their way, and among the most ingenious devices cranked out by this worthy department was a small light gas mask, by now in a well-advanced state of testing and development. One day a burlap sack arrived containing some twenty little masks that looked like toys for playing war, and the colonel, visibly moved, had them brought immediately into the trench, where he stayed for hours on end waiting for the Silesians to launch a few canisters of gas, and sure enough no sooner was the wind blowing strong enough in our direction than a punctured canister comes rolling down from the enemy heights, and to the great satisfaction of our enemies and still greater satisfaction of our colonel, it keeps coming closer and closer, bouncing on the stones, so close in fact that if the colonel had been able to he would have reached out and pulled it into his own trench. But at that point the wind stopped and the gas in the canister started rising straight up, so in order to test the masks the colonel had some twenty peasant boys about eighteen years old put them on and prepared to send them running in groups of five into the midst of the fumes. The first five went forward, holding hands as in a kind of dance, and when they came in contact with the gas you could see clearly that each had broken loose from the others and was trying desperately to remove his mask, and the result was that they fell on top of each other while even the Germans got to their feet astonished and unable to understand this new tactic by the Italians. The colonel dispatched the next five with the categorical order not to remove their masks, and indeed the patrol advanced with great caution and stopped for a moment before entering the cloud of gas, but the fumes must have got to them just the same because the poor boys were all seen to kneel down together as though dazed, then bend their heads forward, and finally fall face down, while the Germans aimed their binoculars thinking not without justification that this was a new method of execution. The third group of five was given its orders, on the double, jump in the gas, take only a single breath, understand? then back to the base again on the double so that the experts could check the effects of the poison on their skin and thereby perfect the masks; the five took off with great strides as though for a broad-jump contest, except that after the jump they didn't get up again. Then the colonel, after a contemptuous look at the captain whose soldiers had wasted fifteen masks, ordered the officers to demonstrate how to put them on, and he himself set the example by tightening the buckle at the back of the neck of a little peasant from the province of Padua, meek and sad as an ox, who being too tall stooped forward bending his knees and bowing his head to make things easier for his superior. The gloves too, gentlemen, said the colonel, suspecting that the gas was of a new kind capable of penetrating the pores of the skin, and since through the wide lenses of the goggles you could see that five boys had become as pale as wax, he gave them a friendly slap on the shoulder, and with that gesture it was as though he was sending them directly into the hereafter because meanwhile the wind had started blowing again along the ground and while everybody else went sprinting away like frogs to put on the heavy old cumbersome masks with the big iron cylinder on the chest, the five of them kept standing there, their dangling arms and little masks making them look exactly like apes, until the first whiff of poisonous fog made them collapse like punctured balloons. Now the colonel was visibly satisfied because finally he had five specimens on hand who could be placed on the examination table at the Bureau of Discoveries and Inventions and there subjected while still warm, even if in truth they were already ice-cold, to all the various analyses that would make it possible to furnish our army with a very light and effective mask with which to go over the top and on the offensive like cats across the rooftops. All the scientists at the Bureau crowded around the table where the five corpses were laid out, and for a good quarter of an hour they listened nodding to the technical report by the Inventor, who praised the advantages of the new invention pointing out to everyone its lack of bulk, the lightness of the material, the practicality of the little buckle hanging under the chin which would allow the soldier to remove the lower part of the mask for a moment from his face and vomit on the ground if by chance a whiff of vomiting gas were to seep through some interstice, the size of the goggles and their distance from the eyes which would keep the glass from misting over if by chance the pupils inflamed by a trickle of tear gas should begin to burn and steam. After this speech they started to unbuckle the neck strap of the soldier from the Po Valley and immediately noticed that the elastic wasn't tight enough, which meant the mask could have wobbled during the assault charge, then they raised the flap under the chin and saw that the man's lips were blue, for despite instructions this imprudent soldier had breathed through his mouth, thereby committing the most unpardonable error for a combatant, since the breath of the mouth is damp and can clog the filters, finally they separated the upper and lower lips with hooks and saw that the gums too were of a strange color, with purple and yellow streaks, such as you don't even find in those long ill with fever, and were it possible to pry open the jaws and look down the throat with a flashlight you'd certainly find the whitish spots and bruises of diphtheria, since the subject had died of untreated diphtheria. What a pity the jaws were now clamped shut with rigor mortis and that there was no doctor present to verify it all and put it on record, but anyway, gentlemen, the thing is so obvious there's no need for anyone's approval. Moreover the eyes, by holding the eyelids open with a needle, you could see they almost had no pupils, that the white of the eyeball had turned yellow and spread to cover the iris, reducing the pupil to a red dot like a drop of blood. What a mistake to have picked a division stricken by a contagious disease in order to test the mask! It could be tested again sometime later, when the division would presumably be cured, and anyway the mask would be perfected as soon as the opportunity arose. Thus among Serbs, Croats, Tyrolese, Silesians, Hungarians, and Italians the most dangerous enemies were actually the Italians, and they also had the advantage of fighting at home against their own soldiers, who had no right either to defend themselves or to suspect anything. The poor infantrymen and bersaglieri had always to keep one eye out for the Croats, who when the grub arrived speared it on their bayonets and waved it around like the Host to arouse the worship of the enemy, and the other eye looking backward in fear that some officer was coming with a paper in his hand, authority on his face, and a new bee in his bonnet. After three years there was no other solution except for all of them to come to an agreement and pretending that nothing was the matter go secretly back home, leaving the officers with all their medals and decorations, who when the enemy shows up are always the first to slink away, to fight it out by themselves, Italian officers against German and Slav officers. But how were they to come to an agreement with their enemies, who instead of speaking expressed themselves by grunting and neighing, and like the mules of the Alpine troops ought to have been marked by a red bow on the ear to show that they bite and a white bow on the leg to show that they kick? When the Alpine troops arrived that had been assembled at Vicenza, where divided into companies they had proceeded on foot slowly across the city in full battle gear, singing funereal songs as though they were already dead and from time to time shouting in chorus as one man, we're the Julia Brigade and they're marching us to slaaaughter, so that as they went through the streets people closed their doors and windows as though a funeral were passing, when these fresh Alpine troops arrived at the front and occupied the communication trenches on the left, while the whole infantry was shifted to the right, squeezing in to fill the spaces left by the dead, the first thing the new arrivals did was to take out their provisions, first warming the bread by holding it between their legs inside their underpants, because it was so cold that by the time your urine had traveled its arc and hit the ground it had turned into ice pellets that rolled around your shoes, and no sooner had the Alpine soldiers started to gnaw their crusts of bread than the wily Croats were standing in front of them, hoping to catch them off guard, snatch the ration, and take to their heels; then an Alpine soldier who had roused himself in time and jumping up had succeeded in grabbing the enemy by the feet and rolling with him in the snow, frisking him here and there trying to find his bread, when he got up felt something warm in the middle of his face, which astonished him it being so cold, and feeling with his hand he realized his nose had been bitten off and there was nothing left but a red hole. So how could you come to an agreement with those dogs and mules? All we could do was come to an agreement among ourselves, and anyway by now everyone was so much in agreement that when Sette tumbled down a slope and in tumbling formed an avalanche with himself at the center of it, realizing with great relief that there was plenty of air in the avalanche because the snow wasn't all that compact and you could breathe well enough inside it and stay hidden, he made a little space for himself by squirming around with his neck and shoulders and closed his eyes so as to sleep for a day in peace and quiet, and as soon as he felt the avalanche slipping here and there because his comrades coming to look for him were poking it with shovels, he was annoyed and the minute they uncovered his head, the head of an aged youth, he looked his liberator in the face and said cover me up, and the other understood and covered him up again, thereby making him a present of twenty winks of genuine rest. When he decided to come out, Sette found himself on a small hillock with trenches but no trees, from which he had a magnificent view of the valley shining in the sun and smoking from a few chance explosions echoing here and there, the echo returning from all sides of the horizon, and down in the plain he made out two parallel dirt roads, tiny as a pair of water snakes, husband and wife, warming themselves side by side in the sun. Except that the water snakes were really moving, two long uniform and solid stripes that wound around curves and set out with determination on the straight roads, preparing now to cross the ridges and pour down into the cities of the plain, toward home. Sette shook himself a little to throw off his last doubt, then tried to imagine whether it would be easier for him to return home without orders or to go and get orders, and immediately he realized that the effort of thinking was unbearable and even painful and that to go home could only be very complicated, and so he looked around dismayed because there was nobody left in the trenches, neither from our side nor the enemy's. So there he stayed, sobbing and forsaken, waving his arms and every so often wondering aloud, now what do I do? what do I do? when suddenly a military courier comes panting in from the left, looks around in a daze, and asks, where's the outfit? Gone home, answers Sette, sitting in his usual place in the trench, and the courier departs on the double and returns half an hour later with another one, who asks, where's the outfit? Gone home, answers Sette, sitting in his usual place in the trench, and the couriers depart on the double and return half an hour later with a third one, who asks, where's the outfit? Gone home, answers Sette, sitting in his usual place in the trench, and the three couriers depart on the double and half an hour later return with a fourth, but the fourth is a commander with a saber in his hand and pointing it from afar at Sette he yells, gentlemen, as you can see, the brigade is at its post, whereupon the four of them vanish toward their fate. To Sette it seemed like an order and since he had to respect it he stayed in his lair, scavenging empty tin cans from which he scraped whatever food was left with his knife, and frozen maps which he licked, tasting a little edible grease under the ice, and even a few pumpkin rinds and a handful of potato peels and a lump of sugar, so that by putting it all together there was enough for that day, and as for the next day, some saint would provide. During the night he waited for a German to crow cock-a-doodle-doo, for a Croat with a face like a shovel to rise up against the moon. His whole body was drowsy and slept, except for his ears which were cold and transmitted the cold to the middle of his skull, where the two colds from right and left intersected and amplified each other, and his bleeding eyes hurt from the effort of peering into the darkness. So when a Croat stood up in front of him and, strange, very strange, shouted cock-a-doodle-doo, Sette tried to shift himself on his legs but his legs were asleep, he tried to shout in his turn but his throat too was asleep. Nor did he even know what to do to command his right hand instead of his left, because he was holding the bayonet in his right and the hand that extended itself instead was the left, so perhaps it was better to withdraw it and put it back in his pocket so as not to irritate the Croat, who was good-natured and could be seen to laugh, or rather could be heard to laugh because he had hidden himself down below as though trying to dig up a few potatoes with his fingernails while a flaming splendor bloodied the sky with huge spots as though a giant whose hands had been cut off were shaking the stumps with the open veins spurting to the height of the stars. You could smell the odor of fire or maybe of blood, or rather it was an odor of fire and blood, that is to say an odor of war, because war, ah, now he realized it at last, is made up of smells, and if you took a blindfolded man and brought him to the front, he'd sniff and say, I'm at the front, and if you brought him into the barracks, he'd sniff and say, I'm in the barracks, and if you brought him to the hospital, he'd sniff and say, I'm at the hospital. But there's another smell that we all know but have never smelled, and which comes after the smell of blood, as though it were, for instance, the smell of rotting blood, and that is the smell of one's death. And all of a sudden Sette's sleeping nose was awakened by a whiff of that unbearable smell, and he leaped, stretched full length with legs spread and arms extended, for instead of being on his feet he was prostrate because he had been caught by surprise and tied with ropes at his wrists and knees, and he felt as though he were nailed to the ground. Unable to move his hand, he tried with his chin to touch the cross he wore around his neck, but the clever bastards had ripped his cross off to make him completely powerless and it would do no good for him to recite the prayer under his breath if there was no God nearby to hear it, and then at the end of his whispered prayer he heard a loud cry and at the same time understood that he'd been the one to cry out, because now the Croat was looking him right in the eyes with contempt, while the German with his left hand was feeling his neck like an expert, searching for the right vein, and following along with the right to cut his throat from one side to the other. When the German figured he'd found the vein, he pressed it with his left forefinger so as not to lose sight of it, but the Croat, who was eating a raw potato, motioned to him that the blow should be struck lower, and he indicated lower by moving his head very slowly like a ruminating cow and chewing his words as though they too were a raw potato that he was unable to swallow. The Croat had the potato in his throat and he had the blade in his, but he didn't feel any pain because his throat was made of rubber and let itself be cut to the bone which instead put up the last resistance, and he too put up the last resistance and yelling desperately jumped to his feet, his knees creaking and arms outstretched in broad daylight, and looking around he had the impression of seeing things as through a pair of binoculars, and the idea astonished him because never in his life had he had a chance to look through binoculars. Everything stood out in great relief, real and at the same time so disturbing that you immediately think it would be better to be someplace else, but since there you are, all you can do is try to persuade yourself either that these things don't exist or else that you don't. Sette therefore recited a prayer aloud without meaning to, but it was only a trick to keep from acknowledging that he was now a prisoner, since the whole army that had passed and was passing and was advancing from the horizon in order to pass was not ours but our victorious and invincible enemies, so light on their horses that they went by silently without disturbing the dead, who seemed to be laid out in full view in clusters as though to serve as ornament and decoration for the parade. Watching them advance toward victory, Sette had no feeling of envy or admiration, on the contrary it seemed to him all of a sudden as though victory and glory weren't all that different from death, and that the great light enveloping the column of cavalry that had just crossed the pass at the horizon to descend toward the plain, festive with bivouacs and bonfires, was similar enough to the great darkness into which he and the other bersaglieri had penetrated that night when they went to seize an uninhabited village, fanning out here and there and running madly and scaring each other and later whooping it up completely drunk from the horrible uncertainty as to whether they were still alive or already dead, and after the drunken spree realizing that the village that they'd been supposed to take was another one. So once again Sette was left disappointed, because the Germans and Slavs hadn't understood that for them as well the direction to take was the one toward home, to spade the vineyards and drive away the blackbirds that eat the grapes, and because of this mistake they too could say they had lost everything, while on horseback they boldly pursued the Italians fleeing through burrows and trenches like rats through tunnels poisoned with sulphur.

3. *A soldier's pay*

On his way home Sette soon came to a village and decided to go through it, but right at the start he found his path barred by a sprightly and jubilant priest standing with outspread legs, wearing a wide cassock and with a gold aspergillum in his hand, while at his side an altar boy held the basin of holy water. The priest must have been there for some time with his hand raised ready to bless the advance units of the Austrian army; the minute he saw the Italian he made a gesture of uncertainty that quickly changed to anger, and stamping his foot on the ground he ordered, get going, get out of here. Sette couldn't run any faster than he was doing already and continued at his usual pace, till on one side of the road he saw a window flung open and a woman with a rifle took a shot at him. As he ran on, the ancient suspicion crossed his mind again that the Italians try to do you in so that they'll have less mouths to feed. When he reached the other end of the village, he skirted the edge of it and when he came upon a big low house sitting on low ground and hidden by the fog, with all its windows half-closed and in each window a crouching cat and with the yard full of dogs that all woke up simultaneously and burst out barking at the stranger, he automatically changed direction for fear of getting a bullet in his stomach, but was astonished when from a side door he saw a little blond girl in a long flowered skirt and green apron timidly emerge and run in his direction, holding out in her right hand something that turned out to be a loaf of bread. When she reached him she stopped, and he gazed at her rather humiliated at being taken for a beggar, but on second thought decided it must have to do with something other than a handout because the big dark oval-shaped loaf was marked with a cross in the center and the little girl holding it up to him kept nodding yes yes with her head, and meanwhile tears were running down her chin. Naturally Sette took it while she ran back inside, and the man looking around saw a heap of dry manure that looked as though it had been put there on purpose to sit on, and there he made himself comfortable, munching the bread and with every bite looking askance at the cross. Again the side door opened and a little boy in long pants and a green apron and a cloth hat with a rooster feather on one side came out carrying a flask of red wine and a glass, and advancing slowly with a certain serious mien as though performing a ritual he came and placed the flask and glass at Sette's feet and calmly turned on his heel. There were no tears on his face, but you could see he hadn't closed his eyes and was badly in need of sleep. Sette kept taking alternate mouthfuls of bread and sips of wine, and every so often looked at the side door in the expectation that a piece of roast pork might come out too or some boiled beef or chicken stew. But no hope, the door was as though nailed shut and the whole house had resumed that smoke-blackened and godforsaken look that you find in Friuli. So Sette got up, stretched, and started walking away, when all of a sudden all the doors of the house opened and out came so many people it seemed impossible there could be that many inside, and they lined up by threes in a not very orderly way, all in little green aprons and knee breeches, and at the front of the line there suddenly appeared a coffin on a cart, and in front of the cart two horses decked with ribbons, and in front of the horses a priest with a book in his hand, who as soon as silence permitted blessed the people and began to recite the litanies, walking with slow steps and followed by the crowd, which expanded and contracted like a huge snake, while over them all hung an air as vast and sad as a hospital. Sette confusedly connected this funeral with the offerings he had just received, and feeling that somehow he was implicated in the mourning he crossed himself three times and set out for home, walking, walking, walking, till he came to a village where the people no longer spoke Friulian, and then he finally realized that he was out of the war. He sat down to rest only for the minute or so it took for a couple of thoughts to emerge, and the first one that came spontaneously to mind was that the provisional life was over and he was going back to the everlasting life, and the second was that the Germans were marching toward his house and sooner or later they'd get there.

4. *The white friars*

After the she-man's arrival the sun shone every morning on a new misfortune, and if I'd been it I'd have refused to rise or have anything more to do with mankind. One morning before dawn the slender colonel, whose name as we later found out was Lembke, arrives by jeep at the Bevilacqua castle, a red cube with a tower at each corner, and smoking a cigarette pauses in the middle of the main hall, which is high and with a net stretched below the ceiling, and there under the net a trapped swallow was fluttering with slanting wings and cries so shrill it seemed to be tearing the net. Lembke, who was in a good mood, raised his smooth-cheeked adolescent face to watch it and moving his eyes from side to side attentively followed its flight, pleased when he realized it couldn't get out. But then the light filtering down from the top of that dark well brought tears to his eyes, weakened by nervous insomnia, and he began walking with quick anxious steps along the square perimeter as though he too were an animal caught in a trap, and as he walked he kept one hand clasped in the other and both of them behind his back and his cigarette clamped between his teeth, the way beginners do when smoking in secret, until he got tired of walking like this, and pausing found himself at the foot of the spiral staircase leading up to the walkway that runs around the battlements. Standing at the foot of the stairs, Lembke seemed to be thinking, or listening, for his mouth contracted and he pricked up his ears in expectation, though there was nothing to be heard but the sharp cry of the trapped swallow, then lifting his gaze and closing his reddened oversensitive lids over his suffering eyes, he stayed there with his chin raised like a blind man well attuned to the world inside himself but who always assumes attitudes toward the outside world that turn out to be mistaken. Finally the colonel ascended one step, then two more, and stopped, finding himself at the level of the first window, which is purposely placed high above the floor so that the friars can't see the world, which anyway is of much less interest to them than heaven. From the third step however you could look out, and what the colonel saw was a blond ess ess boy walking among the dripping fir trees and the flowers of the courtyard with bowed head, carrying his cap by the visor in his right hand, and looking worried or sad because the colonel was late. Lembke enjoyed being able to spy on his friend secretly, and blinking his eyelids he realized with a feeling of pleasure that the burning sensation in his eyes had abated and his gaze was resisting the light, and so he stood there for a while staring at his friend who kept wandering among the dew-laden trees and occasionally slapping his cap against his right knee as in a fit of impatience. The situation was all the more pleasing to the colonel, who turned away and looked around with a truly and visibly happy expression. Now with renewed energy he walked swiftly up the stairs, while four ess ess followed ten steps behind him, quickening their pace when he quickened his, stopping when he stopped. He reached the top of the castle, where he could be seen strolling behind the Ghibelline merlons, surveying the earth like a lord, and making plans, followed by his escort of armed men who kept trying to understand those plans in advance in order to put them into effect even before they were uttered. Having made the circuit of the perimeter, Lembke found himself back at the starting point, and there he saw three side steps leading down to a low and narrow little doorway such as might have been used in the Middle Ages by the lord's dwarf buffoons; he opened it and saw a room too small for a person to stand in it upright. Indeed the person in it was sleeping, or rather he was in bed but with his eyes open, and he didn't seem at all surprised by the visit, as though he'd been expecting it for some time. His insolent look nettled the ess ess who would have like to run in and seize the man and throw him out of the bed, but they were unable to get by because Lembke was occupying the whole doorway and had actually lowered his head to peer inside. The colonel gazed with interest at the walls, the heavy wooden bed, the prie-dieu, the crucifix, and the candlestick, its lighted candle almost wholly consumed, a sign that the friar had been awake all night. The narrow little window, which looked as though it should frame a face, so aroused his curiosity that Lembke couldn't help going in and opening it to look down, and looking he noted that the room was set against the walkway and suspended in the void like the nest of a large bird of prey. This he found so satisfactory that unwittingly he began rubbing his hands, and coming out he quickly retraced his steps and descended the stairs; on the first landing he realized there was a curved niche, and when he turned the corner he found himself at the beginning of a narrow corridor lit only from holes in the ceiling so small that even though they came from the walkway he hadn't noticed them before. They admitted light, but on rainy days also water, which drained along a small gutter on the side until it reached a hole in the pavement. On both sides of the passageway were tiny little doors without locks, which opened creaking on a series of tiny rooms that were like identical dens, low and square, each with a bed against the wall, a prie-dieu, a lighted candle, and a window scarcely big enough for a face to look out. Lembke was electrified by the discovery of these sleeping rooms, and so visibly excited that now he was actually trotting along the corridor, with the ess ess striding along behind him, their boots striking the floor and their helmets the ceiling, producing a clatter that resounded throughout the whole castle like an uninterrupted explosion. The friars, awakening with a start, got up aching and ran to the thresholds of their cells thinking they'd been invaded by demons, which was true, and they watched them from behind thundering along after the first one, who had vanished as swiftly and silently as a cat. Lembke was now running because of the happy emotion of his discovery, which he had made all by himself, no one having pointed it out to him, and stopping from time to time to arrange his uniform, he put his hand to his heart as though to touch and contain its overflowing happiness, and when he passed under a light hole as though under a reflector he raised his face and smiled with gratitude. At the end of the passageway he came upon the curved niche and going around it came out once more on the landing, where he paused a moment to catch his breath and readjust his uniform, also because his blond friend, unable to go on waiting all alone down in the courtyard, was coming hurriedly up the stairs to investigate the muffled roar that seemed to have been unleashed from the bowels of the earth. Seeing him, Lembke smiled, lighting up on the outside and freeing himself within, and actually motioned to him with his hand, summoning him to come and see, and without waiting for him immediately plunged back into the passageway. The ess ess, having emerged in his wake with their helmets dented, had a moment of uncertainty and stopped to give the blond boy the right of way, after which they charged forward with renewed curiosity, for now the tunnel was red and yellow as though a fire had been lit inside it. It wasn't a fire but the candles with which the friars had appeared at the doors of their cells, and from there, without invading the corridor, which would have been blocked, they were trying to get a glimpse of what was going on. And now here again was Lembke, advancing sideways close to the wall and dragging his friend along by the hand, and behind them came the thundering warriors. Lembke has the sinister smile of someone who takes something away from you in order to make himself a gift, and the reason he likes the gift is just because it's been taken away from you and you're left without it. Lembke passed between the two rows of candles with a pinched and ashen face and a fixed smile like that of a skull, and one by one as they saw him pass in front of them the friars took a step backward into their cells, leaving the corridor, once the procession had passed, deserted and streaked with shadows and bands of colored light. The tour being over, Lembke wanted to take his friend into the prior's cell, but after running a few steps he stopped in astonishment, for now the prior, very tall and silent, was descending the stairs with an open book in his hand and a small sack tied to his left shoulder on his back, and without protesting or offering a greeting to anyone he passed in front of the Germans and stopped on the landing, where meanwhile from left and right the friars had begun to assemble, each with a little sack of belongings and a book in his hand, and since the landing wasn't big enough to hold them all, they lined up to left and right on the staircase, one every two steps. The prior went on reading and turning the pages, and as he began each new page he slowly made the sign of the cross over it. Having reached the end of the chapter, he closed the book and put it in his pocket, then raising his eyes to the friars he counted them in his mind, and as he descended the stairs they all fell in behind him, proceeding toward the portal, then across the courtyard, and out into the road that leads to the hills, until they finally disappeared in the distance. Thus Lembke and his men found themselves masters of the castle and they took possession of it by immediately raising the flag over the main tower. Lembke chose the prior's cell as his sleeping quarters and his friend the first cell in the corridor, and the ess ess dispersed themselves along both sides of the passageway like cockroaches, while the lower rooms served for meetings and interrogations and torture and the large hall with the dying swallow became the death chamber.

5. *The walled-up scorpion*

The castle from which the ess ess emerged each morning, buzzing through the villages on their motorcycles like wasps, and to which they returned in the evening coming back from Degora and Tre Lupie, was like a lair from which a scorpion sticks out its pincers, and if you absentmindedly put out your hand it grabs your finger and digs in with its stinger, no matter how much you jump up and down shaking your arm and hit the creature by knocking your hand on the wall, it hangs on furiously till it's shot all its poison into you, after which it releases its grip and lets itself drop and still wriggling with fury and with its tail curled up, drags itself into its hole and hides there. All you can do now is let your finger suppurate around the bite, burning the flesh with the flame of the acetylene lamp, and if it hurts you can hop up and down on your feet, but don't blow on the flame because if it goes out there's nothing left but to cut the flesh with a disinfected penknife, and I won't guarantee it will hurt any less. Besides the flame hurts more afterwards than right away because while you're burning your finger it swells up like a doughnut, and the nerves paralyzed by the fever don't transmit the pain, so in the end you don't suffer all that much and meanwhile the poison is blocked inside and turns to gangrene which will ooze out at night in the form of pus. Now it's your turn to have fun by getting some mortar and a trowel and plugging up the scorpion's hole, thus walling it up alive underground till it gets so desperate that after three days in which it goes crazy and starts chasing itself in a circle, it ends up poisoning itself with its own sting. Lembke too had to be walled up in his castle, and in order to isolate him, with his jeep and his motorcycles and his ess ess so that, having no other outlet, they'd kill each other, the best method of all the ones we discussed with Remo in the Swamp seemed to be to blow up the bridges, all the bridges on the plain between the Adige and the Brenta, in a single night, by coming to an agreement with the partisan brigades hiding out in the Euganean and Berici Hills and the swamps of the Polesine, while reserving for ourselves the bridges of our village and of Bevilacqua, Frassine, and Rovereto. To let the higher commands know about it, we sent a courier to Barbarano on Monday, and he returned on Friday saying it was all right, but that it must all be done at 10 o'clock on the night of 18 October. That left only two days and a night, and so without wasting time or taking a lot of precautions Flash and Skeleton set out with a cart to get the explosives, which were buried underground behind the Hill of the Madonna so that their bitter-almond smell wouldn't be detected, and transport them directly to the Raganella area, burying them right under the river bank, while the Ranfolina squad stood guard, ready to shoot anyone who might happen by. It was a hundred kilos of dynamite, in bundles of small two-hectogram sticks, and after working with them you shouldn't rub your eyes with your hands unless you want to go blind. Our company split up into squads, one for each bridge, each squad composed of two demolition men who were supposed to plant the explosives and a seven-man armed escort. Each squad departed for its destination in the evening, and the one that fell to my lot was the Bevilacqua bridge, right under the castle windows, all of them dark except the highest and most isolated one from which Lembke enjoyed gazing out every so often at the stars, placing himself full face and then in profile as though he were not himself but someone who was looking at him and who must obviously enjoy looking at him since he kept changing position as though for a series of photographs. The understanding was that the demolition men would sleep under the bridge like a couple of vagrants, waiting for an unusual bundle to come floating down the river, kept afloat by a raft of sticks that could be caught with a pruning hook and pulled ashore: that bundle contained the explosive, you see, ready for use. When we got to the bridge there were already two old folks under it, a man and a woman, seated back to back with their asses in the wet mud, they'd each opened a paper bag and were taking out tiny morsels of food which they put in their mouths with a broad gesture of the hand, working their jaws and the muscles from forehead to neck like some silent old disconnected piece of machinery that's no damn good any more. After several minutes of this effort the morsel was still solid and intact, and when they tried to swallow it whole it got stuck halfway down their gullets. This made the old couple, flushed by their exertions, suspend every other activity of their hands and bodies and concentrate all their energies on the throat so as to swallow the lump which on its way down seemed to make their windpipes and eyes bulge so much that for some reason they stuck out their arms. But once the food was down, the operation of swallowing began all over again and so did the jostling of their bodies, each of the two waggling his or her spine as though scratching it on the other's ribs. These old folks didn't seem put out by our arrival, they were content to go on moving their silent toothless jaws like limp curtains, and as for ourselves we weren't bothered by them at all since we had to keep an eye on the baskets and boxes and carcasses of geese and ducks that came floating down the river. The geese always had one wing up as though saying goodbye to the world for the last time, the ducks on the other hand went by with their wings spread like a halo, their bodies flat and their necks going straight down as though the last fish they'd hooked as it went by in the water, transparent as a shadow or a piece of glass, had been too heavy for them to bring up and by remaining attached was acting as a counterweight. At a certain point we hear a motorcycle backfire two or three times above our heads and see it standing with its engine idling and its headlight out, and on the motorcycle observing us a German helmet, and the minute we realize we're being observed the two of us start rubbing our backs against each other and the German, reassured, steps on the gas and goes away. Who knows why this back-scratching gesture should have convinced the kraut that we too were a couple of poor vagrants, since he couldn't have understood the reason for it, and in fact I myself, before I tried it, had though it was a nervous tic, and instead it's a way of warming the body, and anyone who doesn't know these methods isn't really poor. Just in those few seconds I was able to straighten out my ideas on poverty: being poor doesn't mean being penniless or hungry or cold, being poor means being the child of poor people who were the children of poor people who were the children of poor people, and it was your ancestors who taught your grandparents how to live as poor people, and your grandparents taught it to your parents, and at this point no one has had to teach it to you since you were born with that teaching in your brain and immediately started behaving like a poor person without even thinking about it, just as a newborn puppy opens its mouth and finds it natural if a bark comes out and that he's functioning exactly as he should. The poor man lives, of course, but there are three ways of living — living, living big, and living small — and his way is to live small, a pale sort of living like someone who lives in dim light and amid a certain dampness that penetrates through his pores into his bones and swells his joints till they creak with pain, which is why the poor begrudge useless movements and keep everything within arm's reach, until the inflammation even gets into the eyes, which get covered with a dirty yellow film and no longer see beyond the nose. And since the poor aren't able to buy glasses, and anyway don't even know they exist, they all behave a little like old Pernechele, who though he had eight or ten children didn't know himself how many there were because the rascals never told him their exact number. Once in a while he'd have liked to know, just out of curiosity, which son it was who'd come in the house and greeted him as he passed like a dirtier shadow in front of the dirty light from the windows, and getting up his courage he'd stop him by sticking out his cane and with upraised chin ask, so are you Joani? I'm Cen-te, Joani would answer, accompanying the three syllables with three little raps with his knuckles on the shining pate of a father who had lost his wits. Being poor means working as a caretaker to the count, who supports only you and not your family, not even your wife, slim and lively as she is, so she stays in the village while you go to the estate, but you'll be allowed to come home for a visit every year at Christmas, and so as you approach your house along the usual roads, you see a dozen or so unfamiliar kids running around playing in a field, you look at them one by one as though recalled by instinct, and you dwell on the last, who's unable to run because he's a little lame in the right leg — or is it the left? — and meanwhile your fat and sloppy wife comes out on the road to meet you, walking with a great sense of fatigue as though dead on her feet, not even lifting them from the ground as though she had wheels instead of feet, and as she comes up to you she listlessly ties her black kerchief under her chin and in a voice that sounds fearful of the reply asks, did you bring me the money? and you point to the lame child who you didn't know was lame and ask in your turn, is that one mine? and she, already resigned and full of solicitude, goes and picks him up and puts him down at your feet and you raise his trembling chin with your hand and say to him to cheer him up, I'm your papa, silly, and when he looks up at you, you see he's cross-eyed and that means he's really your kid. There's no way out, and as you understand there's no way out, you also understand that you're really poor. If I were writing dictionaries like the ones the teacher has and keeps open on his desk, because every so often someone comes by and asks him to read a letter and if he doesn't know a word he looks it up to find the meaning, well, I could explain what a poor man is better than anyone else. Others say a lot of things because they don't know how to describe the situation, but I'd just say: a poor man is a man who has no way out. Come to think of it, I've just had a better and more intelligent idea, but one that my fellow villagers wouldn't understand too well, and here it is: a man is poor because his ancestors had no way out. Right? Right.

I was jolted out of these thoughts by a nudge from my comrade's elbow, as a box covered with branches came floating down the river, and so that we wouldn't miss it Remo had stuck a vertical branch on top and made sure the edges were a foot or two out of the water, which made it easy to snag it with the hook and pull it ashore, guiding it into a calm little open harbor between our feet. Here we opened the box and counted the contents, everything was there. We examined the bridge. The bridge is made of iron, with two high parapets and a gravel bed, but under the layer of gravel there's an empty space and under the empty space a grid of sheet-metal plates; I don't know why the bridge should be built this way, but it's as though it had two beds, and there's enough space between them for a thin man, like myself for example, to crawl on all fours, with pliers between his teeth and a knife in his fist and pushing a bag with the stuff in front of him, holding it tight with one hand because otherwise, and here's the danger, there were spaces between the sheet-metal plates through which the stuff could slip. I found a support plate of the right pylon and one of the left, using four dynamite sticks for each, tied tightly with zinc wire and with the fuse around it, and let the fuse hang down some twenty feet or so, almost to the water level. It was hard to move, we were sweating. There was a whistle, which meant people were coming, and we froze. We started again, checked everything, then pulled up the fuse to light the end of it and let it drop back down. It was burning without making a flame, and it looked as though instead of burning it was simply turning red. We figured the red end couldn't be seen from the bridge because the fuse was hanging down, but we were wrong because the water reflected the little point of light and even multiplied it with its ripples as though there were six or seven of them at each corner of the bridge. My comrade must have made the same discovery, because I could hear him working frantically and talking out loud, exactly as though he were making a speech and wanted to be heard. In the middle of each bundle of dynamite I inserted the explosive caps and tried to look at my watch. It was 9 p.m. Still an hour to go. At that moment the world shook as though a landslide had started inside it and far away, in the direction of my village, I saw beams of light shining as though a plate-glass window were reflecting an unscheduled sunrise in the sky. Then darkness. Then all the windows in the castle lit up except two, Lembke's and the one in the first cell. I had a vision of the ess ess with their helmets on their heads and boots on their feet, automatic rifles on their shoulders and flashlights on their chests, waiting for Lembke at his door, and since he never spoke no one could know whether he was awake or not. Then I came back to the reality: the bridge in my village had been blown up, and as I stood there crushed, looking at the watch in my trembling hand and with my mind blank, all of a sudden I felt something move in my brain and shift itself from my brain to my eyes and from my eyes go to the watch and from the watch return to my brain, in the form of an idea about the schedule: it was supposed to go off at 10 p.m., but the legal 10 p.m. is 9 p.m.* So I was an hour behind. Everything was done, the fuses were lit and already half consumed, there was nothing to do but crawl out backwards from the bridge and get on the road and from there take to my heels, waiting only a moment to be sure my comrade was coming too. But by now the whole castle was lit up as for a feast and you could hear the electric generators in the courtyard going full blast, while already the first motorcycles were revving up and grouping themselves in fours to depart in different directions full speed as though they were on a race track, followed by a whole formation deployed in a rectangle around Lembke's jeep, which started majestically, crossed the bridge, turned right along the banks, and aimed its headlights in the direction of my village where people were fast asleep in their houses.

---

*The Germans had instituted an hour of daylight-saving time in their occupied territories. (Tr.)

6. *Love and slaughter*

Early next morning two motorcyclists arrived in the village square, helmets on their heads, machine guns on their shoulders, and rage on their faces, and dismounting for a moment they put up on the wall a big white poster with only a few words on it printed in bold type like dirty spots, and before anyone could read it they were already gone. The poster said: NOTICE. Tonight after 1800 hours the Seven Poplars area will be burned down. The population is hereby ordered to evacuate immediately. THE COMMANDANT Colonel Lembke. This is how we came to know the name of the German colonel with legs so thin that the width of his ankles didn't exceed the size of a walnut, and inside that walnut there are two rings of bone, and through those rings pass the rear tendons of the leg, which we at the beginning of eternity will pinch between the nails of the forefinger and thumb and extract, while he, held fast by his blond hair and grasped by the loins, will yelp and howl like a stray dog caught in open countryside by roving boys and skinned alive with a razor blade and splashed with buckets of water so it doesn't faint, and the satisfaction of drawing forth the tendons will be distributed one millimeter for each person, so that each will have the gratification of feeling himself placated to the end of time.

At nightfall a multitude of little German boys about

sixteen years old arrived in the village, wearing overcoats longer than themselves that trailed on the ground, and with frightened and therefore frightening faces, and lining up, half on the right side of the road and half on the left, they began their procession in total silence, as for a holy ceremony. Behind them came the older Germans, who kept steadily arriving in trucks, which they left at the crossroads, falling in on foot for the procession that was on its way to bless the Seven Poplars, and in the middle of the procession, like a holy relic borne high on a baldachin, came the daggerlike face of Colonel Lembke in his silent jeep that seemed to run with its motor off, and at the four sides of the jeep were four German officers who constantly watched the colonel out of the corners of their eyes. When they arrived in the area, at every house they came to the colonel seemed to be remembering a dream or awakening from one, because the dagger illuminated by a dirty light was rapidly transformed into a face, and looking bored and pained he tapped one of the four officers, to right or left of his throne depending on whether the house was to right or left, and the officer thus tapped turned into a beast, sprang away like a mad dog, and bit the ranks of the procession, which broke up with a great shout and scattered all around the house like furious hornets, then jumped in through the windows and doors, and to see if there were people stuck their bayonets in the beds ripping the mattresses and in the wardrobes piercing the doors and in the kitchen cupboards and through the curtains of the understairs, and always running through the bedrooms and leaping down the stairs and in their haste bumping into each other time and again with a clang of helmets and a rolling of their empty white eyesockets, then they came jumping out of the windows and while four of them stationed themselves at the corners of the house, the others ran back to resume their places in the procession. Thus the parade as it advanced lost four men for each uninhabited house and five for the inhabited ones, for example the Ranguttan house, which had been built of mud bricks baked in the sun for only a day so that when it rained the walls crumbled and little holes appeared, letting in draughts of air that eddied around the chimney of the fireplace, and on rainy or stormy days when the air is heavy, the smoke instead of rising through the chimney settled and flooded the rooms, and the family unable to breathe had to move outside along with the oldsters and children and cover their shoulders with sacks, in the Ranguttan house with all those holes and cracks, which children and weasels had enlarged so as to be able to go in and out easily with their bellies to the ground, they were able to do without windows. In fact the windows had either never been there or else having made them the bricklayer, realizing his mistake, must have stopped them up with mud or ox dung, which is also used in winter to seal the holes in the shutters in all the houses so that the breath pumped by our lungs doesn't get wasted but stays inside to warm us. In this house the Germans proceeded less boldly in the dark, hugging the walls with great caution and calling out to each other so as not to get lost, till suddenly amid their words a cry of rage was heard, although actually the Germans when they speak always emit cries of rage as though the mere presence of the person they're looking at makes them fly into a fury, but this cry was different from the usual ones and now rushing out of the many little rooms and crannies the ess ess glimpse an old man seated in an armchair with a piece of wood in his hand, which he had used to hit a soldier who had been circling around him without seeing him. Old Ranguttan is dragged outside on his armchair, violently huffing and puffing as though the effort of removing him was being performed by himself in person with his own strength, they deposit him outside next to a wall and a few feet away they leave still another soldier to guard him who never takes his eyes off him, in fact keeps his gun trained on him, while poor old Ranguttan groaning with the exertion bends down from time to time to pick up a handful of mud and then has such difficulty straightening up again that each time it seems he won't make it, and starts plugging up some hole in the wall, lovingly smoothing the plaster with the back of his dry bony hand as with a trowel. After a little of this hard work, Ranguttan sits back in his armchair, and you can't understand why he doesn't fall on the ground since the hole in the cane seat is bigger than his shriveled backside which resembles a swallow's, but obviously the old man knows the shape of the chair and of his own backside by heart and instinctively finds a slanting peg on which to prop his bony old buttocks, and there he sits with his head resting on his hands and his hands resting on his stick and the stick stuck in the soil between his legs and one leg afflicted by a nervous tic going up and down intermittently as happens to a horse when it's been whipped for no reason and unable to resign itself keeps pawing the ground with its hoof while its shining blue eye turns red as though a blood vessel had ruptured inside. During the search of the house some of the ess ess have discovered the pigpen, and the animal on being aroused pushes its snout through the wall and amid a crash of dry earth re-emerges on the other side and takes flight, but after two skips and a jump its blood, released from perpetual immobility since the animal was cooped up in a hole smaller than itself, starts streaming through its veins with a great sense of vigor, but because the right legs are a little longer than the left the animal keeps running in circles and when the blood floods its brain like a hot dripping cloth the vigor becomes torpor and its eyes close and the animal falls heavily to the ground and goes to sleep, its legs in the air, between dozing old Ranguttan's shoes, in the midst of a world it's only just discovered. And so the two of them, their heads lowered, motionless as sentinels, keep each other company in silence, awaiting the sentence in front of their dens. At the Tanar house they found Tosca still in bed and carried her out into the yard where they put her down on the bare earth and turned the bed over on top of her and jumped on the boards and three of them sat on it and bounced up and down just to make her suffer, and at the Rampazzos, Princivalles, Trafegos, and S-cionas they found the heads of the families at the door of the house and tied their hands over their heads and their legs at the ankles and then hung them from the chain of the well, lowering them down until their heads were just above water, while they yelled pull me up you murderers, but it was useless because the procession was leaving, thinning out as it went along, until only the little German kids were left. Colonel

Lembke seemed to have become cheerful all of a sudden, he was smiling and fidgeting about like a playful boy, and though he never opened his mouth you could see he was on the verge of saying something, and had he spoken at that moment he might even have said something pleasant, I mean pleasant for him, and now and then in the jeep he took his knee between his hands and pulled it toward him and rested his head on it as though overcome by too much fatigue, or as though he couldn't remember why he was there and what mission he was supposed to carry out. When they arrived at the last house and the procession came to a sudden halt and the jeep's engine was turned off, he straightened his neck and his gaze, as though he'd been caught thinking something that should have remained a secret, and since the officers standing at attention were waiting for orders, his lips became pinched with anger and inadvertently he raised his hand to his forehead as though to ward off a headache and with his head nodded yes, then since he already had his hand raised he took the occasion to smooth by rote the curl sticking out from under the visor of his cap, and so doing he moved a few steps in the direction of the blond ess ess boy who had been looking at him for some time, smiling every so often and then looking serious and then standing as though in expectation. Now Lembke was walking with quick nervous little steps, his hands behind his slim backside and his head bent, and it looked as though instead of walking he was simply gravitating around the boy like iron toward a magnet. The boy stood motionless and engrossed, while two corporals knelt over a radio in the middle of the road and turning the crank transmitted the order for simultaneously setting fire to all the houses. Immediately billowing columns of black smoke began to be seen near and far, swirling as though the green vegetation were slow to catch fire, and at the same time a few strangled cries could be heard from nearby ditches, and while groups of ess ess went charging off with their lumbering gait to find the bandits who'd disobeyed the order and hidden themselves in the vicinity, Colonel Lembke shook his head, no, no, looking almost as though he wanted to stop his ears, and turning his gaze to the side he met the furtive glance of the boy, who dropped his eyes. Then moving closer and by now oblivious to everyone, Lembke stopped right in front of the boy, and as though overcome by despair put his head on his chest, first raising his cap and releasing his wavy hair, and the other clasped him in dismayed obedience and with one hand smoothed that wayward curl, then dragged him in an embrace a little to one side as though to lead him out of the circle of onlookers, all of whom turned suddenly on their heels and with their pale washed-out eyes wide open refrained from looking, and away from the fire and smoke and wailing and the whole scorched and stricken world. The wind was dispersing the houses across the plain in sparks and ashes, as the blazing fire rose in spirals, first destroying the attics and roofs to open a path to the sky, then spreading out at the bottom to engulf the walls and conceal them completely, and when it opened out the walls were no longer there. Meanwhile the men who'd been lowered into the wells and abandoned there were suffering pain that extended from the wrists through the arms and skipping over the head passed through the armpits and flooded down their bodies especially along the shoulder blades to become knotted like a lump in the guts, which weighed like a stone. The head was left outside on its own, supported on the shaft of the cervical column like a floating pumpkin, and only the nose suffered as a new pain starting from the nasal septum passed through the bone, setting off sparks each of which was followed by a short circuit in the form of a sneeze. During the first hours Rampazzo, Principalle, Trafego, S-ciona, and all the other men lowered into the wells had tried to climb up the round sides by pointing their feet, tied by the ankles, against some ledge or the branch of a bush growing inside the well at water level and populated with frogs, and by curving their backs against the opposite wall they were able to raise their stomachs which re-emerged from the water like a soaked sponge, but immediately this unstable position made them roll sideways and fall back, in an inexplicable dream that would have been a kind of endless journey had it not ended each moment with a wrenching pain from wrists to shoulder blades. Anyone passing by chance across the yard and hearing the splashing in the water and the sounds of sobbing and gasping and thrashing about would have thought that not one man but a whole family or herd of animals had fallen inside and that each one was struggling to climb over the heads of the others. In the end the men, wheezing like oxen, rotated on their curved spines to shift the pain, and as they pressed their foreheads against one side and the tips of their toes against the other their flesh produced two quivering arcs on the surface of the water and their eyes looked at their own reflection a centimeter away, and in that position I'm sure that each must have understood that he wasn't going to die by drowning or freezing but simply by going mad, and as they looked more closely at their mirrored images they saw their ideas evaporating around their temples and spinning in the air, like a sort of whirligig that brushes the surface and sweeps away even the smallest insect and tiniest grain of sand so that nothing remains but absolute solitude. For the men at the bottom of the wells suffered less from the penetration of the water, their bound ankles, or from hanging by their wrists from an iron chain than from the fact that when they shouted the shout rose up through the barrel of the well like a bullet toward the void of the sky and no one either on earth or in heaven answered them. The breath that came out of their congested nostrils and was heard by their water-clogged ears produced a strange sound, as though between nose and ear lay the distance of a dream, but more distant than anything were their hands because the wrists sheared by the chain no longer communicated with the hands, which when the men looked upward at them seemed to be detached and resting on the upper rim of the well. Their bodies, submerged in the icy water, shivered with tremors that collided with each other and redoubled, while only the brain stood fast, like the end of a spring implanted in something solid. But after some hours of thinking about itself, the brain felt a fog seeping through it that escaped through the eyes, and the upturned eyes with motionless lids like dented metal shutters watched the flitting passage of transparent horseflies with glass wings, until finally a horsefly dropped with its sucker feet on the circle of the iris, and now hidden beneath its large shadow the staring eye no longer saw anything, and the dying man's brain observed the flow of eternity passing silently and unchecked like water through a basket.

7. *Thirty thousand slaves*

At dawn we were back in our hideout in the Swamp and took a head count, no one was missing. Remo had left couriers in the villages so that we could hear as soon as possible what Lembke was up to. Thus we learned that the colonel had visited the village in great silence, going back and forth in his jeep through the sleeping little streets, and now and then making a sign to the officers sitting beside him who were taking notes, tracing the map, and designating houses. Moreover Lembke had left a platoon of men in the main square, connected to the castle by radio and a telephone: the telephone wire had been laid down by two peasants who had been routed out of their beds and forced into the yard, where one of them was furnished with a pack saddle on which a large roll of wire was loaded, which as he walked unwound along the edge of the road, and the other with a pole with a forked end with which to pick up the wire from the ground and place it on top of the hedges; they were led by two Germans smoking cigarettes on a motorcycle, and when one roll of wire was finished the beast of burden had only a moment's pause to get rid of his sweat, dancing around on his feet and shaking his head as though he had a wasp behind his ear, before a new roll was loaded on the saddle and the motorcycle started off again motioning him to follow. Meanwhile Lembke had visited all four villages where the sabotage had occurred and was furious because he could no longer use the most convenient bridge to re-enter the castle, namely the one I had blown up, but had to make a detour through my village where the bridge hadn't been destroyed but had buckled slowly and settled in the water, and after a peasant had been forced to test it by driving a cart over it drawn by two oxen, first empty and then with a load of stones, and it was noted that the bridge could still be used for the transport of loads up to about fifteen quintals, Lembke's jeep crossed it by applying the brakes as it descended and then zooming on the upgrade as though every time he came into view of the wreckage Lembke was overcome by rage. We also learned of a decree that had been posted in the four villages and which read as follows: NOTICE. West Padua and East Verona Zones. As a reprisal measure for the destruction of the bridges over the Fratta and Frassine rivers, the German Command orders: 1) that a man be hanged at each of the destroyed bridges, the body not to be removed until after two days of exposure; 2) that the entire village population is to contribute materially to the reconstruction of the bridges; 3) that each family and all public agencies immediately turn over any material in their possession that can in any way be used in the reconstruction of the bridges, i.e., beams, planks, wheelbarrows, pliers, iron, etc., and that all such material be put at the disposal of the Todt organization; 4) that each village pay within 3 days a fine of 5 million lire; 5) that each village assign shifts of 15 persons at a time to guard its bridge, such persons to be held responsible along with their families.

Each municipality printed broadsheets calling on the

population to participate in the work; the notices were immediately signed by the mayors and distributed house to house. Thus all the men began their long comings and goings between their homes and the bridge, with all sorts of tools and material, for interminable days and weeks on end, and they started by making calculations, mixing mortar, collecting boats, and sounding the depth of the river, the consistency of the bottom, its solidity, and the type of river bed, for there's a yellow clay bottom which is soft for a few centimeters, then hard as a rock, and with clay you can make raw bricks and build houses with the certainty it'll take five years before they get full of holes and crumble in the rain, and with the clay they scoop up from the bottom by lowering a bucket with holes into the river children make themselves ammunition for their slingshots, putting a sliver of lead inside so it keeps its direction against the wind, but for certain stretches of the river there's sand, soft as water, and if you lower a pole it disappears without meeting any resistance, and on that kind of river bottom you can't plant the supports for a bridge. The village populations moved in great disorder up and down the river banks, and where the line engaged in the reconstruction of one bridge ended the line for another bridge began, which meant that from my village to Bevilacqua to Frassine and Rovereto there was one endless chain of people proceeding with an uproar that equalled their fear and never stopping for a second, because the German guards were on the lookout to make sure that nobody was idle or standing upright, and therefore everybody instinctively racked his brains to think of work that required him to bend his back, as for example digging stones, carrying heavy objects, pushing wheelbarrows, mixing mortar, excavating dirt; even when they were relieving themselves, I mean urinating, the men stood bent over and almost prone, and this concern seized them all the more when they saw the great cloud of dust looming from afar that formed a halo around Lembke's jeep. It arrived noiselessly while the driver drove straight through the crowd, which cleared a passage on orders from the officers, and Colonel Lembke cut the air with the impassive face of someone untouched by the misery of this world. No one had yet been chosen for the hanging, but whenever Lembke went by people had the feeling that they were nothing, that any or all of them could be picked, and chance was continually drawing lots, and so chance too had to be avoided, but here the difficulty began because the more you worry, the more mistakes you make, and by making mistakes you compromise yourself and before you know it you're dead. Everyone tried to be on time for work without the slightest delay, even to get there ahead of time, but then there was the danger that if on the day they decided to carry out the hanging as a warning to the population they were to arrive early and find just you, they'd thank you for your offer and string you up on a tree. So everyone stayed squatting in the ditch and crept out on all fours the minute they saw the ess ess motorcyclists emerge full speed from the morning mist in order to catch malingerers. The one they kept their eye on most was Ivo, who was tubercular, and when he bent over to lift a stone it was as though a wrestling match were beginning between him and the stone to see which would succeed in moving the other, and the result was always that after curving his back like an arch he was unable to straighten up, even without the stone, and would collapse suddenly, then lying on the ground and with much exertion of his backbone he gradually managed to get to his feet. One morning, from the direction opposite to the one from which it usually appeared, the colonel's jeep comes plunging like a hawk in a nose dive, and noticing right away that there's something out of the ordinary, we say, oh-oh, now we're in for it, because the jeep is all covered with a net, including the fenders, and stuck here and there on the net are small branches of elm and poplar and tufts of couch grass; even the motorcycle escort is camouflaged, because instead of their uniforms they're wearing fatigues with different-colored spots arranged haphazardly like an April or October countryside seen from a distance, even their helmets are covered with nets, and from the holes in the net hang willow stalks and sprigs of camomile as though the man had lowered his head, gone crashing through a hedge, and come out the other side entangled with those trophies. Now the game is up, because the ess ess have parked their motorcycles lengthwise across the road to bar anyone from escaping and taken up a stance alongside them in their huge boots, and with their machine guns aimed at the closest person, who naturally backs away and disappears in the mass, and the mass groups itself in a block and the block is full of the doomed, because right there in the middle without anyone having realized it is the jeep with its motor off and four officers observing the scene the way deaf mutes look at the world or the way you watch a bee trapped under the cork of a wine bottle, and amid the four sits a demon with two metallic little eyes that gleam like two glass beads in the eyesockets of a statue and seem to receive light not from outside but from within like someone going through the fourth day of a quartan fever. The demon's attention rested less on the spectacle of the trembling mass than on an object that seemed curious to it, namely Ivo who there in the midst of all those people was still on the ground next to the stone he had helplessly been trying to move just to show that he was doing something, and in that position he was so to speak caught in flagrante delicto, and looking around to orient himself as to where the danger was coming from he realized the jeep had driven up silently as though trying to take the world by surprise, and he understood, as though it were something he had always known, that the demon, around whom all the officers were struck speechless because he never spoke, was Lembke in person and it was from him that the danger came. As soon as Lembke's eyes met those of the peasant boy they seemed to rouse themselves out of their inner focus and concentrate on the outside world, to flicker over the endless huddled ranks of people as though seeing them for the first time, and then come back to settle on the boy's eyes that were still staring at him, while two ess ess with machine guns in hand approached awaiting orders, and every peasant understood that the thing that had been so feared was now taking place in the world, and each looked at the demon and in looking at him must have understood who he was and having recognized him continued to look for the first and only time from a distance of three feet at

Colonel Lembke, who at first appeared absent then attentive then powerful, when he made a slight movement with his right hand which rested on the dashboard and at that gesture two soldiers threw themselves on Ivo and yelling lifted him off the ground while the commandant disseminated fear all around him because from the wrinkles of his youthful eyes you understood that as he bowed his head in an anguish that twisted his guts he was smiling with the infinitely sad and tortured air of someone who has never smiled in his life, that he was writhing and even bent double with the convulsed and awkward smile of the powerful man who has been wholly disobeyed and has suffered an affront so enormous that no punishment can ever be enough to erase it from history. Seized by the armpits Ivo was carried dangling to the other side of the bridge, where there was a tree, and there he was tied to a rope that all of a sudden descended from a branch, then he was boosted upward to kick only a few times because he was already dead.

The hanged man was left there on the tree for two days and two nights, drooping and swaying, his body stretched and straight except for his head which leaned forlornly on the left shoulder. Nobody was allowed to approach and cut him down even though no guard had been posted, but at night you could distinctly hear a woman weeping while hiding somewhere, and now and then the sound seemed to change direction, as though the woman, without ever coming up on the road and showing herself, kept creeping from one ditch to another, having found a way to move around so as always to see the dead man's face, which the breeze caused to rotate around the axis of the rope. The weeping lasted until 7:30 in the morning and ended so softly that you always had the feeling it was still going on in a muted way and might at any moment rise in pitch. On the second night a family from a nearby village, who were moving to a new house and had to pass with their chairs and sideboard and mattresses heaped on a cart, turned up at the entrance to the bridge just when the whimpering began and out of respect didn't dare pass, but unhitching the mule camped there on the ground for the whole night crouching around a fire, till at dawn the lamentation ceased and men and women were able to pass, making the sign of the cross and with their lowered heads grazing the hanged man's feet. Once the forty-eight hours were over, the sexton received an order to take the corpse away, and with the help of the baker's son Pasqualetto set out with a handcart. This they pushed under the corpse's feet. The two got up on the cart, one hugged the corpse and the other cut the rope above. The dead man was laid on the boards, taken to the cemetery in the rain and buried, wrapped in sacks. Afterwards the boy Pasqualetto always went around with the noose in his pocket, so as to be able to put it around his own neck on all occasions and show people how the rope had cut through the windpipe, and turning it around in his hands he pointed out that it was really a fairly light cord.

On the same day Favaglioni, the sexton of Montagnana, got an order from the town hall to take down the hanged man at the Frassine bridge. When he arrived, he found people ready to help him and also the priest. There they had used a heavy rope. The dead man's tongue stuck out of his mouth and he had been shot in the left ear. He was hanging on the right from the crossbar between two wooden posts marking the entrance to the bridge, and his feet were only a few centimeters off the ground. He had only one black shoe, with a coin poorly hidden inside. He was buried with his rope, which was removed only after the liberation, when the body was exhumed still in a good state of preservation. The Frassine priest told how it had happened. On Friday evening he hears automobiles drive up and park near the bridge. He goes out. Fog, damp, darkness. Two automobiles, a small truck, flickering shadows. Fear runs through him and he goes back inside. He listens. He hears a shot and a question in a loud voice, is he dead? Someone answers yes, and they all say cheerfully let's go. So they were Italians, with the Germans standing by as observers. Next morning a fascist named Fazzin came to see the priest, with the excuse that he was just passing by, but the truth is that the criminal always returns to the scene of the crime. He says that on the previous day Senigaglia had been turned over in Este to be executed on the Frassine bridge. The victim got in the car without suspecting anything, and Fazzin among others kept him company on his last journey. When they arrived at Frassine, he was told to get out, and the moment he put his foot on the ground he looked around frightened and understood what was happening. One of them went into the first house to ask for some rope, to measure the bridge he said, and a fascist leader suggested calling a priest, but the German in charge indicated no without speaking. The victim stood there in silence, surrendering himself to his butchers and praying first in a low voice, then aloud, and finally shouting as he was led toward the noose, his pants flapping about him as though he had sticks for legs and disconnected joints for knees. The priest confirms the incident that befell a peasant woman who around 5:30 in the morning was walking along the right levee from the Crossing, to meet someone with a cart who was to take her to Vicenza. As she stood on the high bank she noticed in the fog the figure of a man close to the wall of the bridge and asked him what time it was. Getting no answer, she went closer through the fog and touching him realized she was looking at a hanged corpse. It gave her quite a scare.

8. *The exercise of power*

After the torching of the Seven Poplars district and the hanging massacre, whose victims in Bassano were left dangling from the lampposts in the public square for two days, all the villages along the Brenta, the Bacchiglione, the Guà, the Fratta, the Adige, and the Po came out on our side, and if families before had made us pay for food and a place to sleep as though they were restaurants with lodging, and had raised the price if we asked to sleep on fresh hay instead of dry straw, since the dusty straw made us cough which meant a risk of revealing ourselves to some enemy patrol searching the premises, now they received us gratis as though we were members of the family. In many homes large quantities of butter were produced especially for us, by filling bottles with milk just drawn from the cow and then shaking them for half an hour until the milk curdled to become butter and the yellow whey separated and was poured off. This butter was then kept fresh in bottles half buried in the ground or set in the grass, and for the feast of Saint Peter there wasn't a single field that didn't have a row of bottles of butter next to the flask with the egg. The flask with the egg is one of the strongest arguments of faith, because Peter was a fisherman and on the night before his feast if you put a broken egg inside a flask with a little holy water the heavy dew that falls from the sky goes in the neck of the bottle and makes the red yolk take the shape of a boat, with a filament behind it for the rudder, and puffs the transparent white up over it in thin layers to look like a sail, so the result is a proof of Saint Peter's boat. But the families didn't happen to remember the butter until three or four days after they'd put it out, and by then it had fructified, that is to say a lot of sluggish little white worms had been spontaneously born which when you spread the butter on a plate instead of crawling away just wiggled a little bit and then curled up to warm themselves, making it easy to pick them up with a piece of bread and swallow them with gusto. This guarantee of hospitality in every village hugely facilitated our movements the length and breadth of the Veneto because now there was no longer any need to check how much cash we had before leaving, which meant that Remo in his capacity as commander began to live it up and go around the village districts in broad daylight, even crossing the public squares with a long retinue of partisans walking four yards apart each with a gun in his hand so that it took half an hour for all of them to go by. One day we find ourselves in the territory of Merlara and we're walking under cover through a tunnel of vegetation and on both sides of the tunnel we can hear a pack of little dogs whining and yelping as if they had the mange or were making love, and nobody pays any attention, Remo least of all, but when we emerge in the open we get a surprise, it's not a pack of dogs but a garrison of Germans, and since we're standing in the open they throw themselves on the ground all around us and we're surrounded. Remo smiled and walked slowly forward without firing and the German commander murmured to him affectionately, Remo kom, and already Remo was quickening his step to get to him when one of our men disobeyed, opened fire with his machine gun, and killed five Germans (as the inhabitants later testified), but he was left wounded and later taken prisoner and killed with a bullet in the ear. The Germans however didn't seem ready for combat and abandoned the spot on the run, while Remo neither fired nor came to the aid of his wounded comrade, and it looked as though he was very annoyed that they'd fired, and there among his men with their guns smoking he walked around stamping his feet and hitting his hat on his knees in fury like someone who's missed an opportunity, but what kind of opportunity nobody knew. Remo started wandering around with his whole retinue, moving south and west and finally setting up a headquarters along the Adige, and there he did everything to make people notice. It even happened that a certain Zeno, claiming to be a partisan which he wasn't at all because there was no man missing from our group that night, together with four others robbed a farm in Castelbaldo, and the bailiff's sons came to Remo to protest, so furious their jaws were trembling, and Remo was sort of enjoying watching these trembling jaws from close up and even tried to put his finger in the hollow of their cheeks to feel the muscles tensing and quivering, but he soon got tired of the game and lost his temper and decided seriously to hand out justice. He made an investigation and found this false partisan and had him locked up by the brigade while he organized a real trial, then he summoned us all and asked us to vote by raising our hands and the unanimous decision was death. But Zeno's mother had succeeded somehow or other, after a week of going around spying, disguised as a gypsy or a beggar or a field hand, in discovering where her son was being held prisoner and thus where we were camped, and there was the danger she might report us all immediately. When Remo tried to send the woman away, she grabbed hold of her son who was a lot taller than she was, she herself being as small and scrawny as a little girl and indeed her whole body looked like a little girl's but with a death's head on top, and throwing her arms around her son's neck she hung on his chest kicking and screaming like a madwoman. As soon as they managed to separate her from him and take her away, Remo called for a repeat vote and again it was unanimous: death. Remo enjoyed it very much when we raised our hands, and took his time in counting them so as to savor the satisfaction of having a forest of arms raised around him, indeed as he looked around he slowly raised and lowered his head, keeping his lips tight, and he seemed almost to forget the reason we were voting, but assuming a pleased and absent look he indicated that it was all right with him, really just fine, absolutely. In the end he must have started thinking about how to prolong this situation that was so much to his liking. And here was the way to do it: postpone the execution so that in the meantime the condemned man could restore the loot, which according to the victims amounted to 26 sheets, 8 undershirts, 4 towels, 4 shirts, and 20,000 lire. I was assigned to guard Zeno and take him to the places where he'd be able to recover the stolen goods, and for escort I was given Ischia armed with a revolver and two other partisans armed with machine guns. Zeno led us to Via Pegorina in Casale della Scodosia, where he sent for one of his sisters, whispered something in her ear, and then she left. Meanwhile we waited in the house, but more than three hours went by and we began to suspect a trap, so as a precaution Zeno was made to lie down on the floor in a corner of the kitchen with gun barrels aimed at his stomach; another of his sisters was in the house, as well as Zuma or rather her daughter, both sitting on the floor, and at this scene they began to sniffle without otherwise losing control. Finally, the sacks of stolen goods appeared, carried in on the shoulders of some unknown women. Zeno had sent a boy to Montagnana to recover the 20,000 lire, but the money didn't come, and the partisans were worried and fed up. Then Zeno offered two bicycles as a pledge, instead of the money. We consulted among ourselves and decided to accept, and so we left with a sack apiece and two bicycles, and since it was pitch dark and Zeno was unwillingly going along with us to his death, and not exactly appreciating our jokes, always lagging behind though we had him tied by a rope around his neck, we decided to let him go so that we could speed up. When we arrived, the robbery victims were very pleased to see that their things had been recovered and immediately took the opportunity to try on the new clothes, and you might have said the incident was over, but when they counted everything it turned out that four sheets and two under-shirts were missing, having disappeared along the way. Early next morning Remo took two armed men and rushed to Zeno's house, where he found him asleep and arrested him, but he also found Ischia, and being suspicious of him, and since there was no explanation for his presence, he took a shot at him, missing him and putting him to flight across the fields. What seems to have happened is that Ischia had gone to see Zeno's sister, with whom he had fallen in love the night before, but there's no way of knowing because ever since Remo had been the leader of our brigade things were no longer the same, and people did as they liked. Zeno was taken away as a hostage, and now all of a sudden we find a suspect individual going up and down the banks of the Fratta. When we questioned him, he immediately gave his name, proudly and stupidly; I knew him, his nickname was Fart-saver; when we searched him, we found a pistol on him, hand grenades, and a bag of ammunition; since he resisted being disarmed, we had to use force. Tied to a tree with the belt of his pants, the man was subjected to steady interrogation, and readily confessed to being a native of Marega, as well as a fascist, and a fanatic with orders to spy, in the pay of Valeri who was in command in Padua. While we were all thinking it over, Remo kept walking back and forth by himself, and on his own judged the man, condemned him, and taking out his pistol arbitrarily shot him on the spot, to the surprise of us all and especially the prisoner, who opened his eyes wide as he died instead of closing them. That was how Fart-saver, whose nickname came from the fact that he always held them back, was completely deflated in a single moment. He was buried right there, at night: thrown in a hole and covered with a layer of dirt to conceal him from the noses of dogs. Remo thereupon moved his squads across the Fratta, into the municipality of Terrazzo in the area of Verona. Here an accident took place. Verona was more advanced than Padua, and even some of the more remote municipalities, such as Terrazzo itself, already had electricity. After being on the move for two or three days, we find Isidoro's mother in a village, she'd been expecting us for the last few nights knowing that sooner or later we'd pass that way, and she asks for news of her son, but her son wasn't in the squad, and for some reason the rumor spread that he'd had an accident, and so one of the partisans was immediately sent to the high-voltage box in the hamlet of Be Osso, on the other side of Merlara. Starting from there he kept walking under the the wires, following wherever they led, and sure enough he found Isidoro lying on the ground, still alive, and now separated from the broken electric cable that lay close to his leg. Someone said the young man had been amusing himself by shooting at the wires, he wanted to put the Verona area in the dark too, to teach it a lesson for trying to get ahead of the other localities: his shots had cut the wire, which had fallen in the same puddles where he was standing, and the water had diffused the current, paralyzing him. The boy was taken to the doctor, and the Germans guarding the first-aid station let him go through since by now he was dead. In the evening the corpse was taken in a gig to the house of his father, who wasn't prepared for it, the priest having been afraid to tell him, and therefore didn't want to receive this dead son, and barring the door with outspread arms and his head hanging because he was ashamed of bawling like a calf, he kept repeating in a loud voice that he wanted another son. The funeral was held next morning in the presence of the

Germans, and for the occasion the church bell was untied and rung with blows of a hammer, and at the sound of it the people of the village closed their doors while the partisan bands scattered over the plains and the German units reconnoitering in the area went on the alert or moved away in fear of an ambush.

From the moves ordered by Remo it seemed clear to everyone that he was trying to take his remaining partisans back to the woods in the Swamp where they might be safe, and indeed we kept getting closer every night by traveling, half on the right side, half on the left, along the dirt roads skirting the Fratta, in the direction opposite to the current. One night when our men were curled up in a patch of sunflowers and I found myself sleeping alongside Remo inside a rotting wooden wardrobe full of holes in Furiano's hut, we're awakened by clanging alarm bells echoing all over the valley, and we're getting ready to dash out of the trap when we hear voices and see that the hut is full of sweaty seated Germans, and a marshal standing on his feet is leaning over Furiano, sitting on a broken cane chair, and asking him in a loud voice, is having a feast dis village? No, Furiano answers sincerely, and you can tell he's saying no from the motion of his head because you can't hear his voice. Then the marshal puts his hands to his temples as though he were coming down with acute meningitis and opening his eyes more than his mouth, he shouts for some reason in Italian, vee are zurrounded, vee are prizzoners, and rushes out the door all hunched over. His soldiers take out after him like the long tail of a water snake, and the minute they're gone I see Remo, more angry than frightened, hurling curses like someone who's missed an opportunity, but what kind of opportunity you really couldn't tell. To me it seemed clear that nothing could have been done there and it was surely a miracle that it had turned out as it had, because among other things half of our men were on the other side of the Fratta and there was no way they could have come to our assistance in case of a shoot-out. And this immediately gave me something to think about, because it was absolutely incredible that Captain Remo, for he was said to be a captain who'd recently escaped from the army, alert as a fox with his bald skull and whose eyes never stopped moving as though the nerve that controlled them from behind were afflicted with a tic, I say it was incredible that Remo should be caught off guard this way with half his company unavailable, he who in every battle was able to exploit for his own purposes even the reactions of those who weren't involved, for example the peasants and their oxen who by fleeing at the first shot led the Germans to think the partisans were somewhere over there. This man Remo was becoming more and more of a mystery for everyone.

One night Frison, who commanded another group, crosses the Adige under water with two or three comrades to check up personally on this Remo, and what do you know, he discovers the Judas with two ess ess who were pretending to be truck drivers: they spoke to him and Remo shamelessly introduced them to his German friends as partisan leaders, and the two ess ess kept smiling, much amused. The partisans remained suspicious and Frison took it very badly. Kira and Frison immediately went away alarmed and spread the word that everyone should get out of that area. With all the other partisans gone, Remo was left as cock of the walk: early one morning, when the sun hadn't yet risen and the hungry bees emerging ahead of time to drape themselves in clusters on the locust trees were unable to stay up and fell to the ground like stones because their wings benumbed by the dampness were as useless as stumps, Remo with six or seven followers swaggered like a king into Ceo's yard in Merlara, woke him up and roused him out of the house half naked, forced him to untie his horse because it bit anyone else who tried to untie it, made him harness it to the gig, and seizing the reins and whip galloped away at top speed with his cape flapping in the wind like an ancient Roman, and meanwhile Ceo, standing there in the yard with outstretched arms, kept whining and every so often calling out poor Meo, meaning his horse, and poor Ceo, meaning himself. Thus Remo began performing a kind of horse race all by himself, tearing through the villages at noon and in the evening like a bat out of hell, leaning forward over the horse with the reins slackened, and he wore a shirt of red and blue parachute cloth on which was embroidered in beautiful shining letters: Garibaldi Brigade — Commander Third Company — Remo. People in the villages got out of his way, but once he had passed they shook their heads in commiseration and murmured that this couldn't go on. Luckily, after a few days, Remo got tired of his silly game, gave the horse and gig to the first person who came along, collected his men, personally counted them, and reorganized the squads, then after giving orders that each was on his own withdrew unobtrusively into the Swamp.

9. *Half-starved bitches*

The woods in the Swamp are unfamiliar in their depths even to the inhabitants of the nearby villages and only gangs of boys venture across the length and breadth of them in agreement among themselves on the geographical references because they keep a detailed map of them in their heads, having christened with unmistakable names the islets and bogs and sinkholes and hundred-year-old trees that are the forebears of the woods. So when the rumor spreads that the boys from the Farms are castrating a dog at the Pond, the kids from the nearby districts come running immediately and arrive at the Pond by the quickest shortcut, having found the raft made of dry logs tied together with baling wire hidden at the usual bend, and they get on it and cross over and out of politeness send raft and pole back with a push so that latecomers who'll turn up in a minute or two can make use of them, and meanwhile they run toward the place where it's going on, which you can easily figure out by raising your nose and relying on your sense of smell to tell you where the smoke is coming from, there they are, the boys from the Farms, and they've stretched the dog on his back on an operating plank with his four paws held by clamps at the four sides and the exposed belly feebly protected by the tail bent and stiff as a horseshoe, which annoys the surgeon who jabs it now and then with his scissors to get it out of the way, so bloody and dripping it looks like a brush that's just been taken out of a pail. The surgeon keeps the tools of the trade within reach, laid out on a piece of paper, scissors, razor blades, alcohol, pincers, and matches, with the matches you light a fire so as to sterilize the tools each time before using them, and if by chance the fire goes out you can't waste time relighting it, but it's a good idea to have a companion hold the matches ready for the occasion. If the surgeon is skillful, instead of cutting the sack of the balls at the base, thereby making a gash that later won't easily heal, he opens a crack as you do with watermelons to check their color and ripeness, and by working around in this crack he cuts the cord of the balls, removes them delicately, puts them aside on a piece of white paper like evidence, and binds the wound with a white rag that hasn't yet been disinfected because that comes at the end when the clamps have already been loosened but the dog stays there dazed with his tongue hanging out thin and transparent as a used-up bar of soap and doesn't take advantage of his freedom, which he's not aware of till they empty the basin of alcohol right on the open wound, then the animal jumps sky-high with his belly up and turns over in midair, falling back on his four feet, and scurries away belly to the ground, yelping and bloodying the woods and kicking the air with his hind legs as he goes with the feeling of having a burning stick where his balls ought to be. These boys are vicious since they could do their castrating just as well by medical instead of surgical means, the way it's done with young bulls using a specially shaped pincers with jaws like two spoons bound with soft cloth: you carefully take first one ball and then the other in the hollow of the jaws and squeeze while the young bull, held in check by a pincers that grips the cartilage of his nose, can't put up much of a struggle, but shrinks into himself his legs buckling till the balls burst and the bull exhaling a bluish breath, is now an ox cowering on the ground in his own dung with his head lifted upward to the tongs still gripping him and motionless as a dead fish on a hook. Except looking at him you yourself get a twinge between the legs, ouch. Let's hope it never happens to us, eh, man? God forbid, amen. But come to think of it, we did get castrated, when the Germans found us in our hideout, which they'd obviously examined thoroughly and photographed during our absence, no doubt with the help of fascist traitors, who were always ready to oblige them and even overdid it to show their loyalty. One time there'd been a general roundup at dawn in the Brespe district, there was a mist that was more like fog and you couldn't see more than two furrows away, which meant the dogs could be heard barking as they went by but you didn't see the Germans till they were right on top of you, and what happened was that Nanne the lame halfwit, trying to run away because he heard the danger but didn't see it, took the wrong direction and as he went hobbling and skipping along, all of a sudden he made a longer jump and ran right into the arms of a German, who yelling and squealing struggled to get free, finally managing to tear himself away and then fling him to the ground and shove the barrel of his automatic pistol at him, while Nanne kept his hands up and his eyes glowed like headlights trying to find a way out. The German shouted something that sounded like *ammaressaiten ulà ten ponten ista saissa cucca*, which a fascist standing nearby and ready to play the lackey, meaning in this case the executioner, interpreted and translated as take this shit of a halfwit to the other side of the bridge and kill him, the hardest word to understand being *saissa*, which means just what the fascist thought it did and besides perfectly suited poor Nanne, who thereby kicked the bucket and no one ever knew if this was really what the German meant by his order.

Let's keep going, since we're almost at the end. It was really the end that I wanted to tell you about, but the end, you see, is in every moment. A storm is the end, and so is the devil, and so is drought, and war, and so the end could come at any moment, like the Germans. And besides although this, to be sure, was the end, it was only the end of an episode, not the final end. When will that one come? And who will give us the receipt for it? When will we be able to stand on a bridge with someone without being afraid he's going to throw us in the water?

Anyway, we'd been in the Swamp for two or three days, when one night something monstrous happened. Ugh, you can't fight a war with the Germans, since they're descendants of Attila, who was the son of a dog, you'd first have to turn them into men and then fight. There's no pleasure in killing them with a bullet, which must be a delightful death, like a ladder that's been let down from above to allow the just man to start on his way to heaven, but if he's not a just man there's a broken rung and when he tries to put his foot on it he falls. When the count's dog became rabid and bit his daughter on the leg, the count, who understands these things, didn't kill it with a bullet, oh no: he took it out under the plane trees, where the dry leaves hide the anthills, and there he dug a hole and put the dog down in it on its hind legs and buried it with only the head sticking out, and he took a pump and sprayed the dog with milk and then left it there for the ants to crawl up on all sides and swarm all over it biting it incessantly and making it yelp without letup for three days till by then even the eyes had become like parchment and as the parchment cracked it became full of holes and from the holes emerged so many ants that you couldn't tell where they came from. That's the way the Germans ought to be killed, but the truth is that's the way they were killing us, and the Swamp was our hole, its silence and security our milk, and our women, without knowing it, were our ants.

One night, and if hell exists we can say we've been there, one night from our lookout posts in the treetops of the Swamp we hear a woman calling the name Turisendo in a loud voice, and we all got alarmed and tried to keep calm and to hold Torrisendo back by the arms because that was his wife's voice and he wanted to jump down, and after that we hear the woman crying while someone close by her is yelling in German, and then we see that on a path down there they're lighting flashlights to show the face of the woman who looks half asleep and keeps rubbing her eyes in the beam of light, staggering on her feet and reaching out to hold herself up as best she can, and all around her is a flickering swarm of lights looking like a lot of fireflies when they're in heat and their bellies glow, and in the midst of those lights cutting fanwise this way and that we glimpse a uniform every now and then and a pair of boots and a German helmet set on a dull brainless head, and the disheveled head of a woman struggling and shrieking because they're doing something to her. By now we're all in confusion and some of us also take out flashlights and light them in order to move this way or that in our anxiety and so we reveal our whereabouts, and furthermore we now can't put our defense plan into effect which assigned each of us a post to occupy in order to shoot immediately in case of attack, we certainly can't shoot at our women and among other things we don't even know who and how many they are, since they're all screaming at once. So what was the good of going around in triumph through the villages and showing our strength along the tributaries of the Adige? Only a traitor could have brought us to this pass, and now for some reason we're all looking for Remo but Remo's not there, and even before being sure that he's not there everyone's sure that he's fled, we keep saying it to each another, and someone passes the word that Remo is the German with the red flashlight that looks like a reflector. There really is a German who has a red flashlight more powerful than the others, which seems to set the woods on fire and looks just like Remo's, and illuminated by that flashlight the naked women are now running along the path howling like a pack of half-starved bitches and behind them come the Germans in close formation with their dogs on the leash and we all have our machine guns out and would like to mow them down but the women are in front and maybe mine too and so I too do nothing waiting for something to happen, even for the Germans to fire at the women and kill them so that we can attack without remorse. But no one was ready for what actually happened. Torrisendo had always been a little strange, not very courageous, or to put it another way, with a courage that sometimes grew and sometimes vanished. He was always of the idea we should carry out our attacks on deserted roads, not in the villages. In the villages he was afraid for the inhabitants. As a soldier he would have been the kind to stop a whole army single-handed, but he couldn't be a good partisan, the kind who can pretend he doesn't give a damn if you've captured one of his brothers, and indeed makes a show of not knowing him. When they caught Giulio Biscazzo, whom they'd been looking for but whose appearance was so altered by the wild vagrant life he'd been leading that they weren't quite sure it was he, they took him to show to his brother Gino, who along with other detainees had been cooped up all day in the goose pen at the Camons, and sitting there on the ground was smoking a weed and swaying his round sun-burned face from side to side in the sunlight. When they threw his brother, tied to a pole passed under his armpits, down in front of him on his knees and asked him questions, Gino just turned his head impassive as an ox and his eyes rested for a moment on his brother, but to keep from getting upset he didn't even see him, only when he heard them dragging him away for torture with his legs stiff as a paralytic's, did Gino turn lazily aside and bowing his head vomit a little while the Camons closed ranks in front of him so that he wouldn't be seen. Torrisendo, if you please, would have vomited first, and that would have been the end of his brother. But then who can say if it wouldn't be better for the peasants to die, die the minute they're born, and so have done with the whole race of them.

It happened suddenly and lasted only a few seconds: arriving below us, the Germans unleashed the dogs and pandemonium broke out, a barking of animals and a squealing of women that sounded like pigs being slaughtered, and we heard them screaming all our names in confusion one louder than the next and Torrisendo stood upright and grew in height and threw himself down with outstretched arms as though taking wing. He died on the spot, and was the least unlucky of all. A few others followed him. Now there was firing, on both sides, but without order or leadership, the whole company was disunited by fear, and some climbed down to the ground and tried to get away, but there the worst enemies were the dogs, which had been trained to respect boots and bite bare shins. Firing was heard so far away it seemed to come from another village, and instead these were the survivors scattered in a flash to the four winds, without weapons or purpose, and for a long interval there was no sound from the women, then only a few isolated cries. The shooting hadn't lasted long, but there must have been only a few of us left, because those who had jumped down, especially the first, had dropped right in front of the German ambush, that is to say upright at close range. This was what the Germans had come for, they had driven us out of our lair and destroyed us, and we had no other place to hide. Most were dead and the rest, like myself, found themselves in the morning on the outskirts of some unknown village.

10. The Americans

A few people woke up in the night with an inkling that the Mericans were coming, and since the inkling became a suspicion and the suspicion made it impossible to sleep, no one knowing what the Mericans were going to be doing in our parts, they decided to get up and go out on the road and wait for them, but they were in for a great disappointment: night became dawn, dawn became morning, and the horses which had been turned loose in the fields, because otherwise it would have been too convenient for the Germans to go in the stables and pick out the best ones for themselves and jump on their backs and make their retreat in comfort with cushions under their buttocks, after a night of thunder and lightning spent galloping over the rolling plains, now stood motionless on the hillocks with their heads erect and a thoughtful look in their human eyes. Of the Mericans not even a shadow. Not a single airplane, not a single truck, not a single soldier. Who were these Mericans? We didn't really know why they were coming, but we knew that this time we were supposed to await their coming as a liberation, and so there were all the villagers assembled in the square and waiting, strolling around anxiously and leaning forward with their hands behind their backs. Afternoon came, and the throng of peasants, worn out from waiting on an empty stomach, had started walking toward the Fratta bridge to see what was happening farther south. The bridge, held up by what was left of its damaged pylons, looked as though it were resting on the surface of the water, and there, hastily buttressed by new supports and by boats anchored to the bottom, it continued to serve for the passage of pedestrians, though ready to disappear forever underwater the moment the first truck dared to venture across. A hundred yards beyond the bridge, the road curved, and nothing more could be seen in that direction. By now the villagers had lost heart, and some sent their wives home on bicycles to bring something to eat so they could go on waiting. It was necessary to hold out and greet the new arrivals, who in the final analysis are the masters, and in one's own interests try by all means to ingratiate oneself with them. Then all of a sudden, like something out of comic opera, a black man came around the bend in the road: glittering with spangles, wide awake like someone who's just got out of bed, fat and sleek like someone who's always eaten, he advanced indolently with his hands in the pockets of his fatigues, his attention concentrated wholly on his right ear over which, attached to his helmet, hung a little radio broadcasting popular songs. Their surprise and disappointment overflowing, some of the villagers hurled a brief string of insults. No one said it, but each was convinced that this was a mime hired to entertain the little children in some nursery school run by nuns in the vicinity. And indeed, he did a quick dance step to show off before the dazed and unresponsive eyes of the onlookers, then pulled himself together and engrossed in his own concerns disappeared. The bewildered crowd reassembled, again turned its gaze across the bridge, and patiently went on waiting for the Mericans, the Mericans, the Mericans, who were taking forever to get there.

PART THREE

1. *The invention of money*

Every family in the village puts aside its purchasing wishes for a whole year, with the notion of satisfying them after it sells whatever product it may have in excess, and if by chance there's not enough left over to buy anything then the satisfaction is postponed to the next year or even the next without too many complaints. But there are two stages in life when all the wishes previously accumulated come to the fore and are finally fulfilled with the help of brothers and sisters, parents, relatives, well-off villagers, and the priest: these two moments are marriage and death. This is why Jijotto, who had poor digestion and bad breath but had discovered an herb called dulcamara because it leaves a pleasantly bitter taste in the mouth and was always chewing it because luckily he still had two teeth in the lower gum to the right and one corresponding tooth in the upper gum, which meant that his right jaw was still straight and a little longer than the left one which instead was as flabby and wrinkled as an empty sack, Jijotto whom you always saw walking with his head out of kilter like a bucket dented on one side, and who kept in his pocket a bunch of dulcamara stems to sweeten his breath and every so often lowering his head and puckering his mouth he'd take a helping of them from the pocket of his jacket and start chewing, like a draft horse that when the road is straight buries its head up the eyes in the sack it wears tied to its neck, emerging from it with long mustaches of hay, which it slowly sucks back into its mouth chewing them up and swallowing them down into its insides, after having made a little free space by discharging a burst of excrement from behind into the sack tied to its tail, so that the animal, setting out at dawn with a full sack on its neck and an empty one at its tail, comes back in the evening with a full sack at its tail and an empty one on its neck, and anyone who's seen it leave and now from a distance sees it coming back simply has the impression it's walking backwards, Jijotto who in this way had completely reduced the pockets and lining of his soldier's jacket to holes and shreds, so that now he had to carry his dulcamara by tying it up with string in little bundles and squeezing them in his armpits because he certainly couldn't afford a new jacket, and even if he'd wanted to he wouldn't have known how to go about buying it and probably would have asked the town hall, when Jijotto was found dead with a couple of sticks between his teeth and the blissful look of a mouse whose skull has been crushed by the spring of the trap at the very moment of savoring the bait, he was prepared for burial by the Confraternity, and while one washed his feet and pulled the stems from his mouth, another took his measurements for a new suit of dark corduroy, and during the funeral anyone who wanted to could take a look at the dead man through the little glass window in the coffin placed right over the face, and you saw that he was composed and respectful with the flattered look of someone who finds himself in the midst of a group of benefactors, and if it hadn't been for the glass you might have expected him to say thank you, but the glass was actually that tiny barrier that prevents people from speaking between the here and now and the hereafter and exchanging questions and answers, or even only answers since the questions are pointless as everyone knows and the dead can't have forgotten them all that quickly, and looking into Jijotto's face the answer really seemed to be yes and that with his nice new suit he was entering into the beyond with dignity, freed of the vice of nibbling bark like a grasshopper.

Once a month in Montagnana they hold a small market day and once a year, for a whole week in September, a big market, which also serves as a technical exhibition, and you can wander around the neighborhood of the square, dominated by the statue of Victor Emmanuel II who turns his back on the cathedral, and look at everything and take notes and copy the most interesting mechanisms so as to be able to reproduce them on your own if they're not too complicated. Those days are considered a vacation from work and school, and everybody stops to look at the tandem bicycle for two, who pedal together as though they were a single person with four legs; and the double-bottomed rat trap, which works without interruption because when one rat is captured and drops into the lower level it goes on running and uttering cries making its brothers and sisters curious so that they come too and whole generations fall in the trap; and the powder that kills bedbugs in their holes between the bed boards, but nobody buys it because it makes the bugs thirsty and before they die they pour out frantically in single file and suck blood insatiably wherever they can, so that you suffer as much in a single night as in a whole lifetime; the *sgiavare*, which are clogs made from a single block of wood, with no laces, and they're comfortable because to keep them on you don't need socks, all you have to do is fill the empty spaces with straw changing it every two or three days and if by chance you get a sore between your toes or on the bottom of your foot you just soften the wood inside with a little melted wax, when a lone peasant in *sgiavare* passes by along the road he makes such a clatter the women go to the window to see if by chance the German army hasn't come marching back; the magnifying glasses to examine the cracks in the bark on the branches of fruit trees and discover the worm that's making them sick and count the number of its legs and eyes in order to classify it according to species; the blue glass spheres made in France filled with invisible water with a rock in the middle and on the rock the Virgin of Lourdes with her bare feet on the snow, so that by turning the sphere over and then back again you see snowflakes whirling in the sky and slowly settling to mark the contours of things and from the forms that emerge you can tell fortunes, it's a good idea in case of sickness to have these holy spheres in the home because all you have to do to be cured is break them and make the sign of the cross three times with the water from Lourdes; the Czechoslovakian chicken feed with vitamins that turn roosters into capons and make hens lay double eggs; the relief maps of the city of Venice with the houses connected by a network of wires that when you turn a crank gets tighter or looser making the houses sink in the water up to their windows and then re-emerge all the way down to their foundations, and the most amazing thing is to see the Venetian women at the windows who go right on fanning themselves even when it looks as though the waves will spill over inside and wash away the furniture, anyone who wants to try the little Venetian machine can do so by paying a copper for each turn of the crank.

By now life had begun once more and with it the wishes that had slumbered for so many years were revived, especially in the women and in the children who were going to school and seeing pictures of cities in books with all the many details and objects and symbols whose relation to the world they were unable to understand, for example the manhole covers on the sidewalks and the cinema posters that as far as they could tell stood in the middle of the public squares which meant that you could look at them even without paying and get a good idea of them in your head and then think back on the scene and figure the whole thing out, in a color photograph a woman was leaning backwards pushing her hair aside to display her whole face and especially her mouth red as a bleeding wound and a man was standing next to her his hair slicked down with brilliantine, and being a little taller than she he was looking right at her, lowering his eyes to stare at her mouth with a certain intention that had it earned the appreciation of the village would have deserved to be rebuked. As la Mena, explaining her relations with her husband, had put it, all the children he wants, but kisses and hanky-panky nothing doing. The priest was very pleased with this Mena and pointed to her as an example of correct biblical interpretation for the other village women, since for the lack of a big enough bed she slept apart from her husband but every night before going to bed she offered herself to her man and in accordance with the Holy Scriptures put herself at his disposal, asking him without mincing words, Bepi, in the name of the most holy sacrament of marriage, d'you still want something from me? and if Bepi asked for it she just opened a little zipper without taking her clothes off, and if he didn't she could go. When the wheat was sold, and everybody was astounded because the price they got made their heads spin, each family counted up all the wishes that had remained unfulfilled for so many years and picked out the more important ones and looked forward to making its purchases at the big market, and those who couldn't attend delegated the buying to relatives or friends or in the absence of these to the head of the district or some middleman who knew all about prices and was good at bargaining, and so one autumn morning almost the whole village set out by bicycle or in gigs, or on foot across the fields, went past the San Marco cemetery, actually between one grave and another since the cemetery can be said to straddle the road, and poured into the square of the general market in Montagnana, trooping under the gate built by Ezzelino da Romano where a stone shows the insolent tyrant and the mother whose gaping mouth screams her despair till the end of time.

Thirty thousand slaves of our race erected the forty-four towers and four kilometers of walls of the town of Montagnana, working by day in the sun and at night by torchlight, for three thousand days, under the watchful eyes of three hundred officers. The town was built at the orders of the tyrant Zelino, many centuries ago, and instead of transporting the stones from the quarries of Este by cart, Zelino in order not to tire his horses had a better idea and from the quarries to the construction site, a distance of thirty kilometers, he stationed thirty thousand peasants, one every meter, who passed the stones from hand to hand without being allowed to look at the faces of the tyrant's officers who, armed to the teeth, black on their black horses, surveyed the work and whenever it slackened they jerked the reins to make the horses beat time with their hooves. Anyone daring to raise his face and look at the enemy got slashed with a whip, but the worst happened to the boy who raised his eyes just when the white hoof of a horse was seen passing at one's feet at a pace so slow it was as though the rider was trying to take the world by surprise and the boy immediately understood, without ever having seen him before, that this man, followed by an escort some twenty feet behind him and the head of each man in the escort was covered only by a copper coif and he held a pike bristling with hooks except for the escort leader who carried a long staff with a small stiff banner bearing a ruffled eagle, this man was Zelino lean as a cat inside his metal armor with long red gauntlets up to his elbows and his red plume and a glimpse of red cloth swathing his head under the heavy helmet through the open visor of which two metallic little eyes gleamed like two glass beads set in the eyesockets of a statue and they seemed to receive light not from outside but from within like someone going through the fourth day of a quartan fever. As soon as the tyrant's eyes met those of the peasant boy they seemed to rouse themselves out of their inner focus and concentrate on the outside world, to flicker over the endless line of curved backs that came from beyond the horizon of the plain as though seeing it for the first time, and then come back to settle on the boy's eyes that were still staring at him, while all around thronged the slave drivers with bullwhips in their hands awaiting orders and the officers looked on with consternation forgetting to make the horses beat time with their hooves as the work slackened more and more and then stopped completely, and every peasant understood that something unheard of was taking place in the world above their heads and letting his stone drop each dared to raise his back a little bit then a little bit more with ears cocked to anticipate the whistle of the lash that didn't come and then a last little bit until all of them were standing upright and for the first and only time looked into the face of Lord Ezzelino da Romano, who at first appeared absent then attentive then powerful, when he made a slight movement with his right hand gloved in red scarlet which rested on the pommel of his saddle and at that gesture a shock ran through his whole escort and the pikes were waved back and forth and the banner was raised still higher in the calm sky, and at the end he looked frightful when from the wrinkles of his eyes you understood that as he bowed his head in an anguish that twisted his guts he was smiling with the infinitely sad and tortured air of someone who has never smiled in his life, then everyone realized it was all over and the peasants bent their backs and frantically resumed handing the stones to each other, and the slave drivers went back to overseeing them more zealously than ever cracking their whips from behind, and the black knights on the black horses resumed checking the time more meticulously and making their horses stamp their hooves at an ever quickening pace, and while Zelino on his white horse was still writhing and even bent double with the convulsed and awkward smile of one who has suffered an affront so enormous that no punishment can ever be enough to erase it from history, two men of the escort awestruck and quivering with rage seized the boy and tied him to a pike with a rope passed under his armpits and around his knees and in this way they carried him dangling like a piece of wild game disemboweled in a hunting expedition back up the current of the multitude to the stone quarry where four mastiffs were tied up each to a ring embedded in the rock and the naked boy was tied to a fifth ring at a distance such that only by stretching his neck as far as he could would he be able to protect himself, but the boy must have preferred to hurl himself immediately among the dogs just as his mother having heard what had happened came running across the hills by leaps and bounds and shrieking, for on the stone that Zelino caused to be set in the gate as an immortal reminder and warning of his power you see the naked boy with two dogs on one side and two on the other and in the background the poor mother who comes running with her screaming mouth open so wide that it takes up her whole face.

Going through Zelino's gate, the peasants poured into the square and found it empty. Nothing but a few Spanish gypsies who had set up a booth at one end and were selling trained parrots, Padre Pio's prescriptions against sleeping sickness in humans and distemper in dogs, a miniature reproduction of the Madonna of Lourdes, and a bottle of oil that was supposed to make sties disappear when you looked inside it. That was all. As the party of bewildered peasants filled the square, two gypsies hurriedly set up a long narrow bench on which a woman started dancing and showing her ankles, while a monkey wearing a vest made to its size went around with a plate in its hand to collect the offerings and mingling in the crowd was soon unrecognizable, for when in a forest of human heads it too turned its monkey head to watch the dancer you had to have a sharp eye to distinguish the animal from the faces of the people surrounding it. Mamo had a shopping list, but wasn't able to buy anything except the special oil for sties to take to la Onfa who had a child with a big boil on his right eyelid like a drop of blood that wouldn't fall off, and she couldn't send him to the bridge in the early morning to look at the flowing water which would have made the clot of blood dissolve, because as the doctor said the little boy had powdery bones that couldn't support his body and when you stood him on his feet he collapsed under his own weight. So Mamo went up to the counter, pointed to the little bottle of oil on whose label a blue eye with a red sty had been drawn by hand, put it in his bag, and took out his paper money. The gypsy woman took the money in her hand, looked at it, shook her head, and gave it back. Mamo didn't understand. The gypsy demanded the bottle back and called the owner of the booth. They whispered to each other in Spanish, and meanwhile the man's face kept getting darker and darker, then he went up to two or three peasants, made them show their money, said no, no, no to all three, called the dancer and the monkey, sent them inside the booth, took away the bench, went inside himself, and by releasing a string brought the metal shutter crashing down so noisily on the pavement of the square that it echoed like a gunshot. That shot jolted the peasants out of their daydreams and rudely brought them back to reality. They looked around. Victor Emmanuel, tall against the sky, kept his back to the cathedral and pointed at the square with one finger as though to say, here I am and here I shall remain. The houses and windows all around were empty and silent. The booth appeared to be uninhabited, with no sound of footsteps and no voices. Their money wasn't good any more. To tell the truth, no one had ever really understood why in exchange for a piece of paper they should give you rice, or oil, or salt, and there comes a moment when a little country boy, sent for the first time to buy something in a store, is afraid of being laughed at when he takes out paper money. Now here that moment, driven back among the fears of childhood, had burst out, it was now, it was there, as plain as the nose on your face. In fact it must be everywhere, since the gypsies would have traveled up the whole length of Italy from Sicily with their caravan, which probably floated like a great big boat, and were going around shouting the good news, scouring the roads and knocking on doors or going down the rivers and every so often coming up over the banks. The dumbstruck crowd of men in cloaks and women with kerchiefs tied around their weathered cheeks surrounded the booth in consternation, looking at the door that had been rolled down with such a brutal clang and waiting for a peephole to open and the oily face of the Andalusian gypsy to explain the mistake while his quick hand laid out the merchandise for sale to the highest bidders ready to forget about change and small coins. Instead nothing happened, and the fateful iron shutter remained as immutable as a court sentence, about which nothing can be done except to serve it, putting out your hands to the carabinieri who then lock you up, as Trafego did when for the first time he saw two cops coming when actually all they wanted was to ask directions. The two gypsies and their monkey must already have gone to sleep inside there in the darkness as though the drama of the peasants, coming out of the past with their pockets bulging with obsolete coins or a bunch of banknotes folded up in a red snot rag and tied to their handlebars, didn't concern them at all, and indeed they looked just like an assembly of ghosts with their scanty disheveled hair and scabs and eyes left vacant by time conjured up en masse by some witch and who then leave no trace behind except for a few warmish puddles to be understood as the pee-pee of a ghost child with a weak bladder, and this residue of drizzle evaporating in the sun makes the dogs whine and wishfully lift a leg, yelping and pulling on the chain until one of them breaks it in the middle and with one end still tied to its neck and the broken end rattling between its four frantic paws rushes toward the odor of the living dead and there licks the last otherworldly little bubbles over and over again and looks around with baleful eyes: then it's necessary to call the carabinieri and organize the villagers in squads armed with pitchforks and a few shotguns loaded with buckshot, and starting out from the edge of the village to comb the countryside converging toward the central plain where the poor partisans also ended up getting caught when the ess ess burned the vegetation to drive them out of their hiding places, this plain is called the Sleepers because there all those poor souls could sleep who running out of their houses half-dressed and losing their way in the bogs of the swamp and the warm streams from the springs threw themselves face down among the frogs and turning over all of a sudden looked into the face of death which wore a German smile and on its head a helmet with holes for the straps at the sides like the bucket that when it rains the Loony puts on to cover his head becoming loonier than ever because the splatter of the raindrops deafens his ears and his steaming brain can't evaporate but melts and turns to water and his blood turns to mold. Finally the peasants disappeared, first singly then in pairs then in groups and then all of them, bent over their bicycles careening wildly to left and right as though they were drunk or had been to Montagnana to have a tooth pulled, because when you go there to get a tooth pulled and to save money don't want to pay for a shot of painkiller the Montagnana dentist, who's more robust than the one in Legnago, sits you down in his metal armchair and after scraping the tooth grabs it with his pliers and pulls upward with both hands and you're supposed to hold fast to the chair if you don't want to be lifted up like a fish on a line, and it feels like the pain is in your belly because with each pull your contracted guts get stretched to the utmost, now and then the dentist stops to rest and your guts recompose themselves like an accordion when the musician puts it down but then he picks it up again and stretches it out and from your insides comes an unexpected sound that you had no intention of making, finally the concert is over and you go home on your bicycle as fast as you can because if you don't get home in the first half hour you've had it, your jaw swells up and your brain feels squashed and incapable of thought and your squinting eyes don't see very well but have the impression that the whole world is right in front of your nose, and although you may feel all right because the pain isn't much and you can stand it still you're not functioning well and every ten yards you find yourself and your bicycle in the ditch without knowing how it happened, so what you feel isn't so much pain as rage and the desire for revenge and stubbornly you get up and keep going zigzagging this way and that and forcing the cart drivers to get over to one side and leave you enough space. Now when a child has a tooth pulled and gets a fever you put him on the bar of the bike and hold him with one hand, because every so often his eyes which look like the eyes of a dead fish close, and all of a sudden his head drops on the handlebars as though it had fallen off, but immediately he jerks it upright opening his eyes wide and then he half closes them and collapses again and so on all the way home, there you put him on his feet giving him a pat on the shoulder and you give him his tooth wrapped in paper, its two roots shaped like an instrument of torture, and the child looks at it triumphantly so smooth and still bloody and then scratching with his fingernail he makes the first hole he can find in the wall bigger and puts the tooth in it and covers it with plaster reciting in a whisper, wall wall wall wall gimme the hardest tooth of all, and then happy as can be he goes to bed and because of the fever goes right to sleep.

By the time all the stragglers had got back to the village the alarm bells were ringing and yet there was no fire anywhere, nor could it be a flood since it wasn't the rainy season, nor had other dangers or catastrophes been announced in the village at the last mass. Therefore it could only be some unforeseen disaster, like the time when la Mimena on her own had concocted a poison to kill the parasites infesting the scabby bark of the fruit trees and under the skin of the swollen pustular fruits, something that choked their bellies in the middle and made them die of rapid convulsions, and so it seemed she had freed all the village orchards, but within a week nests of ants seemed to have multiplied in the subsoil, winged ants were flying in patrols along the paths and if you raced your bicycle you felt them hitting your eyelids like bursts of buckshot, and la Mimena's husband who had treated his fields by spreading quantities of the poison as though it were fertilizer found himself in the middle of swarms of insects that from morning to night swirled in columns beside the doorposts of his house, gleaming in the shadow, darkening in the sunlight, and it was as though the floor was undermined, for while eating lost in thought with his cap pulled down over his eyes and the plate of watery soup in his hand, at a certain point he'd come to himself and look around, convinced that the plate was actually resting on the floor and he was slowly sinking into the spongy ground because the tunnels had collapsed. What had happened was that the poison invented by la Mimena, by giving the insects convulsions, had squeezed the stomachs of the females and made them give birth, so that for the first time all the infected animal species procreated on the same day and at the same hours, and after a period of time during which people had the illusion that the world had been swept free of parasites here they were back, grown and multiplied, clouding the sky and circling in swarms to celebrate their victory. Not even the priest knew anything about the alarm bells, he hadn't given the order and they seemed to have rung by themselves as they had many centuries ago when cholera was raging in the village and every day claimed a dozen lives, the assembled people were waiting for explanations and meanwhile talking about their money which was no longer worth anything because most likely in Italy other money was unexpectedly and secretly being made. Once again the pope must have picked the wrong letter and accepted the one from the devil, who if only to get the better of him and confuse the world would even have been capable of writing his enemy's name with a capital letter: God. And everyone pulled the handkerchief with the roll of coins and banknotes out of his pocket, and with the help of a pencil sadly figured out how many things he had had the power to buy, until Peloso who had worked a month for Bonomo and been paid with that worthless paper saw Bonomo himself go by, also looking worried and for some reason with his hat in his hand, and so taking him by the arm he stopped him saying, look pal it's no good this way. What's no good? asks Bonomo. My work was good but not the money, answers Peloso, and seeing that the other stands there hesitating, with his mouth closed under his wine-stained mustache, Peloso concludes by saying, give me an IOU or I undo the work. The work Peloso had done had been to build an elevated embankment so as to be able to cross a strip of the Swamp and bring the wagon and tools to cultivate the land that lay on the other side, so you can imagine whether Bonomo would have let him undo it. Instead he preferred to sign a voucher, a sort of ticket that could be used to buy groceries and cheese and products from the pork butcher and various other things to be chosen by the interested party for an amount to be agreed upon. After much discussion, to which the bystanders enthusiastically contributed, it was agreed that the total value would be five hundred eggs and the voucher would consist of ten notes of fifty eggs apiece. Bonomo signed his name in full on each note and thus became the underwriter to make good on the voucher, which meant that if someone had no faith in it and wanted eggs instead of paper he was to go to Bonomo and receive fifty eggs for each note or something else of equal value. Peloso however was illiterate and didn't trust these ordinary and unimpressive pieces of paper, and so he went immediately to the priest to explain it all to him and also to call the priest to witness and, through him, all the authorities all the way up to the pope. He asked that the church stamp each note in purple ink that would be indelible even under the rain, and now satisfied but still doubtful of the system he wanted to inaugurate it immediately and called out to the storekeeper Boccalotto, who was standing there looking on with his flat washed-out face covered with pimples like a piece of Parmesan cheese, and asked him if he could spend a fifty-egg voucher right away. Boccalotto went to the priest for an explanation and then to Bonomo for authorization, and receiving his consent in everyone's presence and the guarantee that at any moment Bonomo was ready to make good on the voucher with fifty eggs or a hen, he tore it off, looked at it, held it up to the light, examined the stamp of the parish, and then followed by Peloso set out for his store to sell the requested merchandise. The example was contagious. Every worker started tracking down his boss in order to get the now useless national money converted into local money, which would be valid forever. Even women neighbors who had contracted small debts and credits with each other, such as a half cup of salt borrowed and never repaid or a spoonful of oil and one of vinegar or a few sprigs of parsley, and until these petty debts were settled they kept giving each other dirty looks and the creditor would hang around in the vicinity of the debtor pretending to look at something else and to be having elevated thoughts, just as a rooster does when he closes in on the innocent hen who goes on scratching the earth and the minute she lowers her neck he takes a leap with the help of his wings and settles on top of her while she squats on the ground under his weight and with a disgusted look waits for the business to be over, so when the debtor would be sitting in the middle of her yard combing her hair in the sunshine and hunting for lice her attention concentrated on her scalp in an effort to feel in what direction they were scurrying and waiting for them with the comb when they got there, the creditor would be skulking along the walls and pretending to water the rosemary or rue by pissing on it or, stone in hand, to waylay the big lizard that with its throat throbbing and mouth raised looks as though it were sucking the warmth of the sun, and meanwhile the sly stalker closes in on the foe and as soon as the latter unawares bends forward letting her hair fall to the ground and running the comb through it to expel the parasites that seize on the slightest little tangle, she lets fly with the stone at the quarry's spine and then grabs her by the shoulders, and planting themselves with outspread legs, head against head and their tongues sticking out sideways, they keep up a silent shoving match without looking each other in the face, shifting their position every so often by a few feet, until after hours of exhausting and taciturn struggle their husbands and children arrive and the scuffle turns into a battle all over the yard with stones thrown and fists and shrieks rending the air; even women neighbors, as I say, thought to dissolve their outstanding debts with the egg currency, and in pairs, debtor and creditor, they bicycled to the priest and there the debtor prepared to issue the money, but being illiterate and unable to sign it, she had it signed by the priest who wrote his own name as well as hers. But for the women another problem immediately arose: the fifty-egg denomination was too large to be useful for their petty debts, and on the other hand the stamp had been used for currency units of fifty eggs and the notes that had been issued were circulating throughout the village all the way to its borders and even infiltrating villages nearby, although such infiltration and exportation of money were strictly limited to cases in which the recipient knew the name of the signatory of the note, was actually his neighbor, and perhaps wanted to receive a quantity of these notes so as to cash them in on a small plot of land that he'd had his eye on for some time. For the women's little debts the priest had a bright idea: he used another stamp, smaller and round instead of oval, which served to validate in the register of documents such collective ceremonies as confirmations and first communions, while the other stamp was used for official documents and marriage licenses and to record deaths and accidents in the village. On the margin of both stamps was the inscription Parochia sancti Salvatoris, and in the middle was a man in a soutane with hair falling to his shoulders, shown in profile, with a banner in one hand and an olive branch in the other; the man was standing in a little boat to show that our parish is located on a river and in the middle of a swamp. It was agreed that the small currency be worth one egg, and that for debts smaller than that there was no need to sign, a person's word being enough. In a later meeting of heads of families it was settled that a whole range of goods not produced by labor should be considered devoid of value and price and therefore left to everyone or to the poorest villagers: such goods included the mold that forms on the walls of the stable from the damp breath of the oxen and which has a healing effect when rubbed on open sores, and in particular on the ulcers that appear on the sides of the mouths of children deficient in vitamins; and the hay that sprouts spontaneously on the edges of ditches and on grassy stretches that don't belong to anyone; and mushrooms that grow by themselves either on the ground or on the trunks of trees where the branches start; and camomile which can be gathered by running a comb along the ground among the stalks and pulling it upward so that when it comes to the flowers it pulls them off intact, allowing you to collect them in a sack tied to your stomach like an apron; and poppies which when put in wine have more effect than camomile, and *bruscanzoli* which grow on the north side of hedges and when cooked in a skillet with a little oil are tasty and crunchy, and in short everything that according to necessity and reason ought not to be considered private property. Instead of replacing and abolishing the circulation of eggs, the local currency increased it: you saw some accounts get settled with forty eggs, partly in kind and partly in vouchers, and the obscene meaning inherent in the word eggs lent itself to lewd remarks about any man who was broke, he's got no eggs, he's broken his eggs, he's lost his eggs, and at this point people looked with obvious commiseration no longer at the man but at his wife whom he was forcing to borrow by opening new accounts. Since the system worked, it never became necessary to convert the money into kind, that is to restore the value of the paper to whoever had issued it, who besides felt himself to be, and in fact was, a public debtor, constantly exposed and liable to be called to account from one moment to the next, and who therefore became ever more reluctant to issue new vouchers and tried instead to corner the vouchers of others, especially those of his neighbors, in the hope of one day being able to demand their conversion into property, choosing of course a plot of land bordering on his own where by displacing hedges and ditches he might further extend his own domain. The most complicated problem arose when the economy of the village was no longer sufficient and it was necessary to start trading abroad, that is to say with the surrounding villages each of which had learned to issue a currency of its own whose real and nominal value was unknown. Lendinara had come up with a triangular currency bearing the image of the Madonna standing on a broad pedestal with her head, surrounded by hundreds of little garlands, stuck high in the upper corner so that the voucher, passed from hand to hand and pocket to pocket, had become so worn and tattered as to be almost round, with the result that no one would trust such money with its decapitated holy image. Montagnana had coined a rectangular currency, with a photograph of the cathedral and the square in front of it, which turned out to be empty, as though the statue of Victor Emmanuel, who turns his rump to the church and with his finger pointing to the ground seems to be saying, here I am and here I shall remain, had been taken away when everybody knew it was still standing there, and so it must simply have had to do with a vendetta by the clergy, which now that the Church had substituted itself for the state, felt itself entitled to ignore the king and take his place; this Montagnana currency wasn't easy to exchange for ours because it had been guaranteed in large part by the sugar refinery and was reckoned for the large denomination in sacks of sugar and for the small denomination in ladles of molasses. So in the beginning our economy avoided trading with Zelino's city, and this turned out to be our ruin because the people of Frassine did exactly the opposite, that is they actually appointed themselves to be a branch of Montagnana by accepting that currency as their own and every month presented themselves at the refinery with a stack of small vouchers asking that they be converted into barrels of molasses, which when fed to the oxen and cows did wonders in fattening them and for the production of grade A milk. Our own economy at this time started gravitating toward Cologna, where a small machine factory had opened, but Cologna belongs to Verona and is some thirty kilometers away with five or six villages in between with a total of three or four different currencies, making it illogical to expect that our vouchers would be recognized and accepted at the end of the world, and therefore anyone on his way to buy something had to convert his money in each village into the local currency, with the result that with each conversion his hoard diminished a little and when he arrived at his destination he had only about half of it left or the machine he bought cost twice as much. This problem put a damper on exchanges with the outside, limiting them to such strictly indispensable things as pharmaceutical and veterinary medicines, since for the time being we had only to survive in expectation of normal times. We heard that the workers in Legnago had stormed their factory because even they had been paid with phony money, but once inside the plant they didn't know what to do and stayed there for two nights having their wives bring them something to eat, then realizing they were trapped like cats in a sack they started throwing things around and smashing them trying to break out, and the result was that the factory was demolished and they found themselves back home sitting at the empty table and looking fearfully at the worthless banknotes in their hands. In our village, the economy expanded a little once the Rabbit launched his system of buying and selling the currencies of neighboring villages, because now it turned out to be easy to convert your own vouchers in advance into those of the village where you were going. The Rabbit got up early and without washing or changing his clothes, since he always slept fully dressed on a mattress of green leaves that with time had become soft as a sponge but also stank from having rotted, set up his table outside his door, a table with plenty of drawers in each of which he kept a supply of currency from a different village, and there he sat with legs outspread on a cane-bottomed chair at the end of the table, his shoulders protected against the cold by a short red cape that made him look like a cardinal, and thus attired waited for the arrival of some stranger intent on spending money in our village or some villager in need of goods from the outside world. After a month's time the Rabbit's operations had become so widely known and recognized and legal that when he ran out of outside currencies he wrote letters of introduction in his own hand in which he attested that the bearer of this piece of paper was his creditor for a total of x number of eggs corresponding to x number of Madonnas, the currency of Lendinara, or sacks of sugar, the currency of Montagnana, or blocks of salt, the currency of Chioggia, and before writing the figure Rabbit checked the amount and its equivalence on a chart written with many flourishes that he kept hanging on the wall and in which all the currencies of the vicinity were provided for. In the beginning the exchange was limited to direct acquaintances, the field hand received the voucher from the boss and gave it back to the boss, but later the circulation was enlarged as the number of pledges increased, because if the recipient didn't know the underwriter he had whoever brought him the voucher add his signature, but even this system didn't last long because the wheel began to spin more freely and the fragile currency, eggs, and the sweet currency, sugar, were going in and out of all the houses and a system so well tested seemed destined to be perpetuated when something disconcerting happened. The Rabbit had had a visit from a stranger who got out of a long black car with a big cigar in his mouth and dressed like a god, in a vest and swallowtail coat and black-and-white striped shoes, one of those who probably go out in the city by night so as not to have to mingle with the disinherited rabble and who demand that offices and stores be opened just for them and put back in order. Who knows what had brought him to that godforsaken village, maybe a caprice or he'd taken the wrong road, but anyway there he was, grumbling and chewing his cigar and showing two rows of very white teeth; laughing repeatedly as though he had a tic he came up to the table and started turning his pockets inside out removing from the linings rolls and packets of vouchers from many different places, not all of them known to the Rabbit and not even clearly provided for on the exchange chart, and what's more he delicately set the top hat he was holding under his arm down on the table and out of it began taking eggs and more eggs. The Rabbit hesitated to pay the whole amount because he wanted first to check the place or origin and the guarantees, but the stranger had darkened like a spent candle and scowling as though he were suffering from a liver attack and making the cigar bob up and down between his teeth, he said, pay half. To the Rabbit it seemed incredible that he'd be satisfied with half, but that's what he gave him and then watched him get in his car and depart swiftly but so silently it was as though he'd forgotten to start the motor. It was only at this point that the Rabbit looked down at the eggs and was dumbfounded because all of them, and there were about fifty, were stamped with strange foreign words and the face of a smiling woman. Never mind the woman, the question was what did the words mean, and so the Rabbit shut up shop, collected the eggs in a basket, and went to the priest. The priest put on his glasses and read. They were English words. He put his glasses back on and deciphered. They were calling Meri Maria. He adjusted his glasses and made one last effort, it said: Meri Maria come tonight —John. A Merican, some Mericans, all the Mericans were calling Maria, some Marias, all Marias. The whole thing was very suspicious. First of all, it meant that somewhere there were the Mericans, God knows where. And that they were involved in the exchange of local currencies, God knows how. And that they were trying to get rid of those currencies, God knows why. It needed to be thoroughly looked into, but one thing was clear: Italy had become Merican, and probably the new money that was on its way was Merican money, the old kind was abolished. In the following week, the Rabbit and all the other villagers stopped working in order to scour the neighboring villages and redeem the vouchers, and when the operation was over every household was left with baskets of decorated eggs and cans of sickly sweet molasses swarming with huge yellow and green flies, and for a month no one ate anything but eggs and sugar until the supplies were exhausted and once again rows of people stood in silence along the sides of the roads waiting for the Mericans, the Mericans, the Mericans. And now in the distance here comes a single file of men dressed in white cassocks, their heads covered with white hoods and bent over an open book, which they're reading so attentively that they don't even seem to see us as they go by, and they must be well practiced in simultaneously reading the same words because they all turn the page at the same moment, and it's only when he's in our midst that the prior pauses a moment to tell us that he's come back so that we won't be left alone and on Sunday he's going to explain our history to us, and on Sunday we're all in church to hear his sermon. So now listen to how our history repeats itself from olden times according to the parable of the friars.

2. The Stone Age

In a year of the immemorial time that lies buried before the memory of each generation a foreign army passed through Italy and history has yet to decide whether it was French or Spanish, and besides it was an army so numerous coming in successive waves that it may well be that the first waves were Frenchmen looking for Spaniards and the last were Spaniards looking for Frenchmen, and that there were also some companies of Germans trying to join up with one side or the other, since for the Germans the important thing is to fight and whom they fight doesn't matter to them. The fact is these armies went by week after week, first in small bands led by some bearded old braggart who only by experience was still able to manage his long pike with its wooden shaft studded with esoteric symbols, tilting it smartly when with a thievish hand he entered low doorways but not bothering much to avoid people's heads; then reconnoitering units that patrolled the highroads and elevated river embankments on swift horses in order to take possession of the landscape with a predatory glance and calculate where the human settlements most worth looting lay; then the bulk of the army, with ramshackle carts that lost a wheel every hundred yards or so, spilling their contents in the mud, whereupon people were roused out of nearby houses and with pikes pointed at their backs forced to reload the rich fabrics and the casks full of wine that the sun and mold had turned into rancid vinegar; then the baggage train, with cages of chickens, bloodied from constantly pecking each other, and dogs with mange under their tails, which not being able to scratch and bite it, kept turning round and round in circles barking furiously at the last tuft of hair that wavered just before their eyes, and robust draught horses, grown old in their passage across Europe from the steppes in the north to the beaches in the south, with withered testicles and the mild eyes of those who have become straw in which death sits hatching its eggs; then nothing; then special divisions, on horses advancing slowly at a rhythmical trot and with a steady rocking of the croup that cradled the dreams of lanky knights who at the end of the day woke up astonished in a different country, and at the end of their lives were to wake up astonished without being sure whether they had campaigned in Holland or Greece, since after so many years they were still unable to tell from the dialect spoken by the wives they had taken from there; and every so often officers who with bright purple cushions under their buttocks went galloping for some reason in the opposite direction, perhaps in a frantic search for their own squadrons lost to view after the last drinking binge and never found again. All this great hubbub of tongues and billowing of dust, which whitened everything from the gravel roads all the way to the distant woods, and cracking of whips and cries and laments and with them the beating of hands* grew into a storm that spun like a waterspout

*Dante, *Inferno*, III, 27. (Tr.)

through the occupied villages and left behind on earth and in the sky an absolute and silent void filled with devastation, since whoever had had a bed had one no longer, and whoever had had a cow found only its head, the eyes bulging with a questioning look, the bones stripped of flesh and the tufts from the tail, and whoever had had a horse no longer found even the crupper, and whoever had had a salami found only its casing, and whoever had had a wife was left with nothing but a couple of garments in the wedding chest. And so the village herbalist and the priest and the head of the village assembled the boldest, including the brigand, and marched through the smoking rubble toward the center of the enemy encampment, whose location was easy to guess because from it came such sputtering trumpet blasts that they sounded like obscene jokes addressed to heaven, and there arose from it besides a steady sound of braying and the thick smoke of pyres and the smell of flesh being scorched without having first been skinned and of chickens roasted with their feathers still on. So they arrived there in the heart of the village whose single square is still there today in which the whole history of our race has unfolded over the centuries and where now on the first Sunday of every second month the tax collectors from the bank set up their little table, and there they got ready to ask to speak with the supreme head but no sooner had they arrived than they looked around and realized there was no point in speaking because everything was clear. At the very center of the square two tall poles had been planted like the masts of a ship and between the two poles a rod was tied and from the rod, hanging by one eye from a hook, swung the skull of some foreign king with the lineaments decorated with gold; a dropsical man with a huge flaccid stomach like a half-filled sack had fallen in a hole and being unable to get out was muttering imprecations, sticking out his lower lip as though his mouth were trying to speak to his nose; a screaming naked woman, her hands to her stomach, ran crouching from one tent to another in pursuit of a caparisoned dog; in front of the host's tent a man on all fours kept kicking an empty cask, and farther away, crouched with their bare buttocks on their heels, a group of soldiers crowned with ivy were playing dice; families of rats in single file crawled from one group of tents to another led by the father who made a beeline for the rancid tidbit and swallowed it whole, discharging for his offspring only a little pile of excrement which arranging themselves in a circle they gobbled up; a group of tatterdemalions captured in some nearby village slept between the shafts of a cart, packs tied on their backs and their open mouths swollen from the tranquil sleep of those who when all is said and done have been given something to eat; a short fat man dressed as a woman in skirts and apron and on his head a bonnet with earlaps came sashaying out of the bushes holding a pole which turned out to be a spit and on the spit a pig had been roasted, and after the pig came another man holding the other end of the spit barechested with Turkish trousers and a long horsey face with lips that every so often he drew back as though to neigh and exposing his long prominent teeth. Finally a true commander of soldiers also appeared, with the doglike air of someone born to prevent others from becoming men and who examines them every so often and watches over them to make sure they remain beasts; he sprang out from between two tents with one eye cocked and both ears alert and his hands hidden behind his back, and the minute he spotted the little group of peasants wandering aimlessly around the command quarter he immediately called them over with a shout and led them hurriedly into an open space toward a circular red tent, the finest of all, topped with a gold pinnacle with a little banner fluttering gaily in the wind and twisting in such a way you couldn't see the insignia, and here after a trumpet blast a warrior appeared who was so huge it seemed impossible he could be contained inside the tent, and this is how he briefly answered their complaints: turning right and left he showed his whole enormous chest covered by a scaly cuirass that would have housed three ordinary warriors, and on every scale a letter of the alphabet was written in such a way as to form a sentence, which an interpreter spelled out in a stentorian voice touching the words with a rod:

SO AND SO
ENEMY OF GOD
OF JUSTICE

not to mention

OF PITY.

The giant turned completely around so that all sides of him could be seen and remembered, then bending quickly forward with his hands on his stomach he sighed and retired inside the tent, closing it behind him with unexpected delicacy.

While the vanguard and bulk of the armies were encamped there on the plains of the Adige and Po, settling down with great turmoil and waste along the streams and tributaries, which now ran yellow through the countryside like overflowing sewers, the rear guard still uninformed of the lull caught up with the encampments and bypassed them, and in search of virgin lands to pillage spread southward in the direction of Rome, wriggling through the long entrails of Italy like a tapeworm in a sick intestine when with tickling coils it reverses its direction. And so the leading armies, having become the rear guard and thinking that the order had been given to leave, regrouped and pulled up stakes and with their long baggage trains departed in confusion, and anyone who woke up a few days late found himself on his own and not being used to it roamed whining along the roads in twos and threes or in delirious groups twittering like swallows in search of any leader whatsoever. But despite all this the army was by no means diminished in number by these sporadic losses, on the contrary it was substantially increased by the spontaneous addition of the disinherited from the various villages and by husbands seeking their wives and children who had run away from home and parents who were pursuing them and herdsmen who had fallen in love with mules and horses and their owners, who might also be slave drivers but no doubt looked dignified and mustachioed, accustomed to great power and to creating their own laws like the gypsies, who every time they pass across our land, arriving from Albania or Montenegro with the excuse that our last queen was a Montenegrin, behave as though they own the place and send someone into the kitchen to keep the stupid owners occupied while the others rob the cellar or untie the horse and gallop away on its back calling it by hundreds of names until the animal by perking up its ears shows that the right name has been uttered. Once the Fox wanted to question them, and bounding into his own stall, he woke up the first gypsy woman who was sleeping peacefully on the straw and asked, by what right are you here? By this, she answered, raising her skirts, and so the Fox didn't know what to do. One day some long automobiles with blue curtains and women in litters and men in jerkins passed through the village, and they waited in front of the town hall granting audience and administering justice as soon as any quarrels broke out, but after a few days a Mongolian horseman showed up who wore only a vest over his chest and on his face his mustaches, and approaching the main tent he barked something and in less than no time the company was once again on the march toward Lendinara, where by now there were more gypsies than inhabitants, and the latter began to feel so insecure that they held an assembly to decide whether or not to move to Comacchio where people had evacuated land and houses because of malaria. The gypsies however kept their composure and behaved meticulously according to the rule of honor posted up on the trees, and grouped by nations and languages of origin, France Spain Yugoslavia and above all Greece, since Turkey and Bulgaria heard about it too late and arrived when it was all over, they wept and tore their hair in the empty square. The fact was that Zaira, the international queen of the gypsies, had died after a week of agony, right there in the center of Lendinara, inside her golden tent supported by twisted wooden columns and adorned with the flags of all the nations including the ones that had disappeared from history without giving notice to the world, and shortly before she died in order not to travel by herself along the roads of the hereafter, venerable and delicate as she was, it was necessary for someone else to accompany her of his own free will, and so here and there duels broke out between claimants to the privilege. They fought in pairs with knives shorter than daggers, at a close distance established by the length of a short rope tied to their necks with a slipknot to quell the temptation to run away, and when it was over a circle of spectators with folded arms surrounded a little group of dying men who were writhing in blood that had a strong wild animal odor and calling upon Zaira, until Zaira died too, and then two in front and the others behind accompanied her pale and hesitant shade among the shades of the other world who rose to their feet and murmured their surprise. The abuse of power confers the same majesty on gypsies and invading armies, and thus many peasants assembled and the army would have slipped away more numerous than when it had come, like an earthworm crawling through the swamp that becomes encrusted with mud and dung, if it hadn't been thinned by a great number of deaths, which only now when the camps had been struck, appeared under the naked sky. Animal carcasses and human corpses rotted in the sun, and if you brought your ear close to the bones, the horns of the oxen, and especially of the bulls, you heard inside the buzzing of bees born spontaneously and ready to fly out as soon as the calcium crust had split, and all of them together in the tunnels hollowed out in the skeletons heaped up across the plain were making a racket like a great wind raging from the Adriatic, and it occurred to you by habit to look up at the leaves to calculate the direction of the storm, but the leaves were motionless as though nature too stood waiting. After a few days and nights the interminable humming as of a stalled locomotive became a whistle like a speeding train, and in thick swarms or single file like a self-propelled rope the insects poured out into the open, making a nose dive as soon as they saw some peasant going shirtless through the fields, and now here the poor devil already had cholera in his body and by dropping his pants was infecting the soil. Within two days all the villages were full of bees and wasps and gilded blue green and red flies buzzing amid a great stench over the putrefied countryside under a tainted sky, and the plain swarmed with restless rats as though each drainage ditch were a festering sewer, and the priests from the various villages, followed by an emaciated and tattered retinue, met in the fields to perform exorcisms, each hoping to liberate the area of his authority, and each priest, standing in the midst of the kneeling faithful and bending over the holes in the ground and the tunnels of moles and agilely warding off the swarms of grasshoppers, would say, I exorcize you, pestiferous rats and caterpillars and worms and grasshoppers, on behalf of Almighty God and all the celestial court as well as the Holy Church of God, by cursing you I curse you so that you may be cursed wherever you go and may you diminish day after day so that nowhere may your remains be found except where you may be necessary for the good and prosperity of mankind. But it seemed that from the corrupt bowels of the earth the devils were driving to the surface everything that was filthy, and so after a few days the priest came back with a still more emaciated group of ragged followers and softened the exorcism into an entreaty, Almighty and Everlasting God, grant to us sinners the boon not for our own merit but by thy mercy and do thou curse by our cursing, confine by our confining, and exterminate by our exterminating these pestiferous rats and caterpillars and worms and grasshoppers. But it seemed that God was now fed up with human turpitude and had stopped his ears with tow like a shepherd when he doesn't want to be disturbed by a flock that never stops bleating, and in the end the dead were sure of being dead and the living were not sure of being alive, and they wandered around in the autumn fogs eating the last beets and tubers that the air hadn't contaminated and drinking dew from the palm of the hand because the water in the river and ditches was polluted and poisoned with overswollen carcasses that fell apart in flakes as they decomposed. When two living souls saw each other from a distance they stood there dawdling and perplexed, unable to decide whether to approach each other or not, and in the end each went his own way because neither had the courage to note his own misery from the condition of the other. It was as though, advancing with their brutish bearded faces and seated comfortably on the scarlet saddlecloths of their drowsy horses, the Spanish or French or German officers, or all of them together, had with each step they took set history back one century, and now humanity found itself in the Stone Age, with ape-men wrapped in a few stringy garments that might have been either fabric or fur, with the leathery skin on their faces scorched black, and only the eyes sometimes showing a flash of memory and awareness of their lost intelligence.

Continuing like this, some of the big apes were already walking on all fours and in good weather, when a few trees bloomed spontaneously and the soil yielded green chicory and red berries, there were now men so brutalized that they no longer remembered to feed on them, but sought only warm-blooded animals and set traps for wandering hares or birds that nested in bushes, and when they captured them they took them by the legs and bashed them against a tree and with their nails and teeth immediately sought the innermost and tastiest parts, especially the heart, and sipped the blood from the veins. Thus over vast areas human plagues were no longer to be seen but only animal ones, because man too had become a predator and plunged down shrieking from the trees and flew like an arrow at his terrified victim, who not knowing this new enemy wasn't sure whether to flee from him by leaping in the air or running close to the ground, and in this uncertainty stood there paralyzed until the attacker crushed it between his hands and curling back his lips tasted it with his long yellow teeth.

The books* say that civilization was reborn when man, roaming over the land with his woman and seized from

---

*Giambattista Vico, *Scienza Nuova.* (Tr.)

time to time by the sudden promptings of his libido, was ashamed to exercise it under the open sky, which shuddered chastely and thundered, whereupon refined by his terror he dragged his woman by the hair into a cave and made this his fixed abode; when the earth breathed forth the dry vapors that rose in the air to produce lightning, strong-limbed giants, the last survivors and thus the most robust, scattered through the woods along with the animals that by tradition had their lairs there, were frightened and awestruck by the great effect whose cause they could not guess, and raising their eyes noticed the presence of the sky, which anyway had always been there above their heads, and this was the great discovery that set civilization back in motion, and since they themselves on the rare occasions when they spoke to their wives and children or to the other giants did so in such a way as to express their most violent passions by shouting and grumbling, so they imagined that with the roar of thunder and crackle of lightning someone in the sky was trying to whisper something to them, and ever since for time immemorial man keeps listening to find out what it is.

So man and woman began to live together and as they went roaming toward the horizon in search of a larger and more stable abode they renamed what they saw, and being ignorant of the natural causes that produced events, they gave their own nature to things when they couldn't somehow explain them by similarities, just as today, for example people still say that the magnet is in love with iron: the human mind, wherever it spills over into ignorance, always makes itself the rule of the universe about everything of which it knows nothing. Overweening pride and unrestrained bestial liberty have meanwhile been mitigated because if man in the wild state loved only his own salvation, once he's taken a wife and had children and discovered God he loves his family's salvation along with his own, and so in accordance with justice, family, civil, and finally human society is reborn around the rulers of cities, which for our area means the ancestors of the count's family now living at the top of Monte Salice, whom it's never possible to see from outside since they hardly succeed in meeting and seeing each other, lost as they are in all those salons and long corridors of the castle; and the ancestors of Mea the lawyer, whose house has its own church which means that every Sunday the priest from Scodosia has to cut short the mass celebrated for the people and rush on his bicycle to perform one for the lawyer, who at exactly eleven o'clock is already waiting in his private chapel with his wife at his side and his tenants and sharecroppers behind him, and he's so sleepy that it's obvious he just got out of bed, and in fact the hem of his pyjamas is sticking out from under his trouser cuffs; and the ancestors of Lazzaro, who's the richest man in Badia, and when you grow tobacco he comes to count the shoots one by one and writes down the total on a note pad, and when the harvest is ready you'd better be sure to bring all of it to his drying sheds where the leaves will be hung in perfect geometrical order so he can easily count them when he comes, grumbling and corpulent and giving off that bad odor that makes people remark that Lazarus was rotten when Christ raised him up. All these ringleaders got together and assembling the multitudes organized a vast campaign to go over the great plains of the Adige and Po inch by inch and drain the malarial lands where the cholera had passed by digging ditches and canals so that the surface waters could run off, and thus the Scolo Dugale and Fossa Degora and Vampadore canal and Lungo Majo were constructed in our villages, and in partial compensation for such munificence by those ancient lords it's only right and proper according to the friars that even today the peasants who have escaped cholera and plague pay a tribute every two months to the families of Mea and Lazzaro and the count, who assign the collection of it to those same functionaries of the bank who come in pairs to collect the taxes, taking up their post with two chairs and a small table, and on the table a flask and next to the flask two full glasses which they don't offer to anyone, on the very spot where the tent of the Spanish or French or German commander, enemy of God and everything else, once stood.

3. *The Industrial Age*

The children of the poor got along as best they could by building mole traps, stamping on them with a red-hot iron not their own names but the names of their district, and even without prior agreement it was clear to them all that each would be allowed to go around and lay his traps only in his own district, otherwise the trap would be pulled out of the ground and broken to pieces and left there as a warning. The trap consists of a small wooden board, seven or eight centimeters wide and twenty long, holding underneath it at each end a hoop of iron wire five centimeters in diameter; a steel rod is stuck in one end of the board bearing at each end a loop of thin copper wire and in the middle a string; the rod is bent until it touches the board and the two copper loops and the string are made to pass through three little holes drilled in the board at each end, that is to say corresponding to the iron wire hoops, and in the middle, while the string going through the middle hole is held by a stick, the loops are widened to conform with the shape of the iron rings; now the trap is ready and is placed in the mole's tunnel and carefully hidden with lumps of dirt, for if the mole sees an opening of light that it doesn't recognize from never having seen it before, it gets frightened and turns back, but if instead everything looks dark it keeps going its usual way, feeling on both sides with its pointed snout and sniffing out the presence of earthworms, and by butting its head against caved-in earth and the roots of couch grass it moves them aside and makes progress, and when it encounters the stick of the trap it bites it with its teeth and knocks it out of the hole and so the rod is freed and flies up pulling with it the copper loops which clamp the animal against the wood and keep it there until the boy's arrival, which may not happen for a day or two; the animal, by now dead and stiff, is cut along the belly from head to tail with the family scissors and skinned, and the skin is stretched and nailed to a board and dried in the sun. On Saturday the skin dealer goes along the roads shouting moleskins at the top of his lungs and the boys are waiting at the gates with their stacks of skins, they curse and haggle over the price but always end up selling everything.

The boys who hunt moles are naturally the poorest, they own nothing and can be seen going around in gangs and also making snares for thrushes to be set next to bunches of late grapes so that the bird gets caught by its feet and the more it flutters the tighter the knot pulls, till it stops fluttering for a moment and lets itself fall head downwards, and then it's all over because the blood floods its brain and the bird twitters as though drunk, and they make peahen decoys, bird shapes as though seen from above, and scatter them in the stubble dripping with dew so that the migratory birds think they're seeing others of their kind down there who've been lucky enough to find good feeding grounds, and fluttering delightedly this way and that they descend in flocks and populate the whole terrain, thus becoming a substantial target for gangs of boys crouching in the ditches, who load their slingshots with four rocks at a time and let fly. The mole hunters have in fact acquired the right to exploit all the possibilities for survival far and wide offered by the subworld of violence and abandonment, and when an ox goes lame and having become disabled is wedged between four large poles planted in the ground and felled with a sledgehammer blow between the horns and after the veterinarian, who always goes around in yellow boots and yellow glasses, has examined it and authorized the sale of the meat, the mole hunters come running in swarms and help quarter the animal with cleavers and kick away the dogs and cats, which sniff like locomotives while fighting over the entrails, and they arrange breast rump brain and ribs in full view on an inclined plank so that the blood drips off on the ground, and on behalf of the owner's wife and calculating the weight by eye they sell the meat to all the villagers, who for that lucky day can afford to eat meat, but when the money received exceeds the value of the ox the sale is halted and the remaining meat divided among the poor and starving of the village, who've all been there waiting for half a day curled up on the ground with a basket between their knees.

In good weather the mole hunters join the teams of reapers who cut the wheat and get paid by the sheaf, and they're never turned away, on the contrary most times they're usually sought after not only by the whole village but by neighboring villages as well, except of course for Marega where they're all cannibals and you can't get in anyway except by sabotage. Indeed there's a custom that the first peasant to finish cutting the wheat and binding the sheaves and stacking them by laying four on the ground in the shape of a cross with the ears pointing inward and another four on top and then another four and at the very top just one, placed in such a way that it covers and protects the grain underneath, and because of this sequence of crosses the stack itself is called a little cross and it stands there exposed to the sky like a prayer that storms will keep away or go around it, I say the peasant who finishes first pulls up a basketful of onions from the vegetable garden and singing insulting vulgar songs, with his cap pulled down over his eyes and followed by the ragged mole hunters, jumps over the ditches and makes the rounds of his fellow villagers' fields, and wherever he finds the work half-finished or not yet begun he sticks a pole in the ground and at the top ties a bunch of onions and the wind makes them knock against each another like the balls of billygoats on their way to new pastures. The point is that the juice from the onion is supposed to make the peasant who's behind in his work weep for shame.

On evenings of these eventful days the boys go swimming in the river, as do a few brazen girls, and I say brazen because a good half of the boys go bareass, and you hear them shouting and brawling for one excuse or another but actually just to let off steam and create a nuisance, and the ones who don't know how to swim tie a dry pumpkin full of air on their backs and this way they're able to float and learn the strokes without swallowing water, except when a practiced companion approaching underwater grabs someone by the heel and pulls him down while he has nothing to hold on to and then sends him back up with his lungs half-clogged spitting and squirming with tight-shut eyes, and then he himself dives deeper where he can't be seen and surfaces twenty yards away in the middle of a crowd of heads, so that nobody recognizes him as the culprit and there's no hope of revenge.

4. *Messengers of the storm*

In this quarter century since the war ended our countryside has been hit by storms six times, and these are the events we use to keep track of time: if you mention a year we don't know when it was, but if you mention the June storm everybody knows when it was because it came at the beginning of the month and leveled the crops like a steamroller and for that year it was necessary to postpone weddings and try to postpone funerals too by keeping the old and the ailing alive.

Messengers of the storm are, for instance, the contrasts in light and shadow among the four points of the compass; or the flight of the heron, which has been a prisoner of the rain cloud, and uses only one wing as though the other were broken and keeps twisting its neck from side to side as though about to be struck by a lightning bolt; or the gaze of sedentary birds, which hold their heads not vertically with one eye on the right and one on the left but horizontally with one eye on the ground but half-closed and the other aimed at the sky and wide open as a mirror, so that the hawk will be reflected in it as soon as it invades the circle of the horizon, moving with the force of its shoulder blades as though it were swimming not flying, and then all the birds depending on their degree of fear hide themselves down among the branches or further down on the trunks or still further down in holes in the ground, in alliance with the snakes.

You can feel the storm coming from very far away, announced in advance by infallible signs more obvious to the nose than to the eyes, indeed there's a penetrating odor of still and stagnant water that descends vertically from above and encloses the area that fate has chosen in a padded bell jar of silent menace within which everything immediately stops, grass bushes leaves branches, you hear only peasants running frantically like horses to arrange the cut wheat in the form of crosses, cover the fruit trees, stack the hay, tighten the wires that support the vines, and try to save what can be saved, while those who have fragile products such as tobacco hop around in their yards like grasshoppers, barefoot and shirtless, dragging the carts to arrange them in the shape of a cross on the threshing floor. Meanwhile through the cracks in the now closed and bolted windows the candles that the women are lighting in front of the Madonna shine in the soft darkness, all the other lights in the houses and barns have been extinguished by an atavistic instinct, rooted deep in the soul by the experiences of the war, to seek escape in the darkness and reduce one's chances of getting hit. All of a sudden the river ripples, the trees shake, the grasses and crops wave back and forth in the fields as though unraveled by the first blasts of the storm, which advances across the no-man's land in a circular dance lifting in a vortex everything it seizes and uproots, and parallel above, behind the fleeing hawks and falcons, the whitish leaden edge, thin as a breeze, marking the area in which the scourging begins, is flying inescapably in your direction, and hailstones as big as walnuts hit and bounce on the brick threshing floor which resounds like a drum first with many sounds and then with a single one, and all the women, whether housewives or field hands, file sorrowfully up the stairs and naturally go for no particular reason to the upper rooms where men will never know what they're doing, and immediately the tension is broken also because now the water is coming down in driving sheets and for several feet above the fields nothing can be seen but a white foam within which great havoc is being secretly accomplished, as under the Germans, and in these minutes the men in those lucky villages that have escaped the blow repeatedly fire their guns at the rain cloud to sabotage its ice deposits and the charges explode high up in motionless and useless puffs of black smoke immediately rent by the wind, and everyone thinks with a brutal sense of liberation, it must have hit the Sleepers, the Lowlands, it must have hit Tre Lupie, it must have hit Canal Feudo, Scolo Dugale, it must have hit Degora, and later they'll go rushing off in a flock of bicycles to check, with the stupid eyes of an animal receiving a reprieve, what it is that's happened to you and what didn't happen to them.

When the storm is over the animals come creeping on foot out of their holes and the men on bicycles out of their farmhouses, moving off in different directions in accordance with the instinct that bears them.* From a person's way of riding a bicycle you can distinguish different social levels, for instance, the small direct cultivator, who pedals very slowly, hunched over and always looking at the ground; the tenant farmer who keeps looking at other

*Dante, *Paradiso*, I, 114. (Tr.)

people's fields on both sides of the road because he lacks a sense of property; the livestock and feed dealer, who instead looks straight ahead into people's eyes and always goes around with a stick with which he hits the rumps of animals for sale thus forcing them to change position, the better to see their muscles and calculate their weight by eye; the big landowner, and watch out for him because he's an especially powerful type around here, sanguine with a sturdy constitution sustained by good meat and strong wine, always on hand for rich banquets, the rightful guest at all wedding dinners in his village and those villages where his name is known, slow in pedaling, quiet as an ox in his total tranquillity of conscience which he derives from the priest's docile dependence on him, and who even makes his wife sleep in the stable with the cows and takes the female field hands of the village to bed one after another, and already there are children who look like him running around in other people's families, dull corpulent animal-like children whose mothers' husbands don't dare to mistreat them because he's the boss and their wives tease them by singing, sticks and stones may break my bones but names will never hurt me, and the same clumsy lack of skill with which he advances on the woman's bicycle, pedaling with spread legs to allow his huge stomach and broad groin to expand in well-being in front of the seat, makes him at first sight a natural member of that species of masters priests and pharaohs whose power is great because you can't tell where it begins and ends. The frequent use of the bicycle, motivated both by the fact that it's the most suitable means for getting around the countryside on the various kinds of thoroughfare, which range from grassy culverts to muddy paths to embankments and ditches, and by the fact that it can be easily cleaned even when encrusted with mud because all you have to do is lower it in the river from the bridge by a rope and let the current wash it and the fishes lick it, makes the peasant's appearance uneven, since the right leg of his trousers often gets caught between the chain and the teeth of the sprocket and ragged and full of holes ends up being much shorter than the left, in some cases coming more or less to the knee with a few long shreds hanging further down. You can immediately tell who are the children of the poor because all they have in their houses is a man's bicycle, and not being able to straddle the seat they're obliged to pedal without sitting, bending their bodies generally to the left of the bar and in order to reach the right pedal twisting and deforming their spines in the shape of an S to maintain a perilous equilibrium; indeed they often fall.

There's no question but that humanity is divided into two races: people and poor people. I learned this early, at the time of nursery school and the daily scuffles that went on there between the poor contingent, the children of peasants, who wipe their snot on their sleeves or on their fingers, which they then rub on their pants, and the rich mob, the children of carpenters and school janitors and blacksmiths and plumbers and the like, who from the very first day had humiliated us by demonstrating the existence of handkerchiefs, the first great discovery of my life, by taking them out of their pockets ironed and holeless and blowing their empty noses with a loud honk for the sole purpose of inspiring in us the need to imitate them, so that those prone to yield to the temptation found themselves dripping with mucus and with no better remedy than to make hidden use of the leaves of plane trees, the veins of which scratch your nose and whose fuzzy coating makes you sneeze. In the nursery school the only secret strength that gave us any assurance in defending ourselves against arrogant bullies and protecting the little girls from their harassment was the certainty that the nuns were on our side. One day a little boy, livid and black as a peppercorn,* slithered out of the grasp of the attendants and burst into the girls' classroom, where the mother superior, seated on a stool that vanished under her wide robe, clapping her hands and rhythmically swaying her head, was beating time for ring-around-a-rosy, and bending down and with an effort of both hands without unbuttoning himself took his peter out from under his short pants. All the girls with little shrieks like wounded animals rushed to cling to the nun's skirts and the lay attendants came running to drag the snot-nose away, crying shame and giving him a slap, shame and slapping him again, but the mother superior put her hands to her head, her eyes and mouth wide open, and instead of shouting or scolding, as all of us were expecting and all of you are expecting, she burst out laughing like a madwoman. That day I felt a surprise comparable only to that of the soldier who goes on patrol in enemy territory along with his commander and soon finds himself surrounded and taken prisoner and taunted by his insolent enemies, and the one

*Dante, *Inferno*, XXV, 84. (Tr.)

who's commanding them is his own commander. The matter was all the more serious if you consider that once a month people from San Marco went by with a cart to collect the offerings that were obligatory in the villages from which the children in the nursery school came, and the offerings could be a ladle of white flour or corn meal or an egg or a liter of wine or a basket of fruit or a live hen, but in any case they meant a certain hardship for the peasant families who, poor things, never tried to get out of making these contributions for the simple reason that a long tradition that had come down from time immemorial represented the nuns as spotless paragons, being enormously better than us who live in the world and in the final analysis should be proud to have the honor of supplying their upkeep.

When I succeed in plumbing the depths that lie beyond memory, I see no more than two nuns, one with her hands to her head who laughs like a madwoman while around her the whimpering little girls cling to her robe, and the other who drags a little boy toward one corner of the courtyard where nettles are cultivated on purpose and watered every evening, and she takes off one of his shoes and scrapes his foot over those prickly weeds, losing her temper when he screams, while the other little boys stand around sulking, leaning against each other and all of them against the garden wall.

I don't recall the two events as actually happening at the same time for there are many gaps in my memory of my early years, due especially to the painful experiences that came later and which I've told you about in detail, and which have so to speak sequestered my whole consciousness leaving me without a past or a future, without a past because truly my memories of childhood and adolescence are like visions reflected in a misted mirror from which nothing comes to light except where some drop of moisture makes a peculiar streak from top to bottom and opens a peephole through which, painfully distorted, the image of the human figure filters out; without a future because I always live in expectation of something that still isn't there and probably never will be and I myself don't know just what it might be. It's nevertheless probable that the boy who runs into the girls' classroom where the mother superior is directing ring-around-a-rosy and who by bending down and making an effort with both hands without unbuttoning himself takes out his peter and the boy whom the nun drags toward the nettles where she takes off one of his shoes and scrapes his foot over them to sting him are the same person, and besides the matter seems perfectly consistent from a logical standpoint. Every evening the attendant watered the courtyard of the nursery school including that far corner where the nettles grew, and when at the end of the day she appeared with the pail in her hand we children stopped playing all of a sudden and watched her in silence as she sprinkled away to make the prickles of those nettles cultivated for our punishment grow more luxuriantly, and then we passed dejectedly from the courtyard into the hallway where our parents sooner or later would come to pick us up, those in the village on foot, those from the neighboring villages by bicycle, and among the latter was my father whom I would have singled out among a thousand even in the dark because he smelled pleasantly of dry manure and sour sweat; he'd put me on the bar of his bicycle and all the way home he'd never say a word.

5. *Life everlasting*

And so began, after the world war, a quarter century of blissful life, in which everyone in the village got along all right and the poor were simply poor and not unhappy. As you went along the roads on sunny days you could see poor families cheerfully delousing themselves in the yards, brother with sister and wife with husband, like this: the one being deloused sat with head lowered over the knees of the delouser who went through his hair with a comb and then holding the comb against the light immediately spotted the dark little clot of the louse, grasped it between two fingers to extract it and by squeezing it between two fingernails and rubbing one against the other cut it in two, or if it was too small and not worth squeezing between the fingernails, it was enough to hold the metal comb over the fire burning alongside and scorch the little creature, which shot away and in its flight caught fire with a crackle, tracing a parabola in the air like that of tracer bullets. These vermin thus diminished and almost disappeared, and all that was left was the problem of bedbugs which are bigger and hide not in man's hair but inside straw mattresses where, awakened by the sleeper's warmth, they surround him and invade his whole body and suck his blood with their trumpet-shaped mouths. Indeed the poor are happier by day than at night, and you see them strolling around their muddy yards and squatting beside each other, the old people in the middle, leaning their backs against the wall exposed to the sun, so useless and idle and disinherited and forgotten that they have nothing to tell each other but a few jokes, and they get animated only when the smallest child, taking advantage of his crouching position, has thought it the right time to make po-po, and then the mother takes a shovelful of warm ashes from the fireplace and covers the excrement. As night falls the poor unwillingly enter their houses to go to bed, and they don't say let's go to bed but, because of the bedbugs, let's go get bitten, and their night's sleep is broken up into half-hour intervals because every half hour, when the poor man has fallen asleep, he feels a needle piercing him behind the ear and then ever so calmly, so as not to let the bedbug big as a cockroach get away, he gives his whole cheek a violent slap with his open palm and while his ear goes on ringing he feels the little trickles of warm blood in which the creature has burst and dissolved flowing delightfully to his chin; half an hour goes by and the man is already snoring blissfully, his lips so swollen with sleep he looks like a horse, when all of a sudden he kicks in the air as though he were having convulsions because one of these little creatures has got under his armpit and inserted its proboscis which has multiple openings for its extra satisfaction. So in the morning the poor, their bones shattered by sleep and their veins swollen with fatigue, get up and cluster smiling and half-naked around the fireplace, where the old woman has already rekindled and lighted the fire, starting it with coals in order to save the matches that among other things she doesn't have, and under the ashes she's heated to the cooking point an onion, which will be given to whoever yesterday had an egg, an egg, which will be given to whoever yesterday had a squash, and a squash, which will be divided among those who yesterday had an onion, and after the morning meal here they are back in the sun under the low wall infested with lizards, which also bask in blissful idleness.

Cente's sister, whose name nobody knew because nobody had ever heard her called by name and she may never even have been baptized and registered at the town hall, ate dirt and shat mud, and since she was half paralyzed she walked on all fours trotting like a bear cub and quickly getting tired, and when she got tired she'd stay bent over with her head to the ground, holding it between her hands, her legs outstretched and her backside bare, since in her house they didn't know the use of underdrawers, and she'd linger in that position to catch her breath, or reverse her position by lying with her bare backside on the cool earth and her chest up, looking proudly in front of her and surveying the world from ground level. With this system Cente's sister never moved far enough to go out of the yard, and you could tell from her muddy excrements where she'd dug the food for her last meal; if it was sand, she'd eaten in the inside corner toward the fields; if it was black soil with a few earthworms, she'd eaten in the shady corner under the wall; if then there were little pebbles it meant she'd gone too close to the road and had to be scolded so she wouldn't go out in the middle of traffic, because if she were to go out on the road and were to stay there for an hour or so and by chance a cart were to go by, the driver might well think she was a pig and, instead of slowing down, speed up and run over the little creature, and if he were to carry her home, realize only when it was too late that he'd probably killed a human being.

Old Temeno, being a paralytic in a wheelchair, had gradually learned to push it by himself so as to be able to go about a little in the fields, but one evening he made a wrong turn and fell into a ditch full of frogs, which went splashing away from him on all sides while the thin wheels sank in the mire, until he was left with only his head sticking out, which he kept turning from side to side, getting more and more worried because toads and green flies were alighting on his skull as though he were already dead, and indeed little by little the cold invaded his brain and he preferred to sink blissfully underwater and have done with it, feeling a pang in his heart because his family would never find the wheelchair. The most fortunate of all was la Belana, who had sold her field in order to be admitted to the hospital, to a little room that had been fixed up next to the toilets, where under her pillow she kept a spray deodorant in order to purify the air and breathe it clean in large gulps, and there after three days of constipation she died serenely with folded arms and a smile on her lips like someone who's fooled the world, except that while the nuns were taking her away, lifting her up by the arms and legs, her constipated bowels loosened and the corpse evacuated along the corridors until the good sisters abandoned it on the nearest table, overcome by such a fit of laughter that they had to hold in their guts with one hand on their stomachs and with the other stop their mouths.

It used to be that the dead were taken to the center of the

village where all the relatives had been waiting for an hour, lined up along a track of beaten earth, muddy, slushy, almost impassable even for goats, and so dark and narrow with the trees closing over it that it seemed like a tunnel. This track leads to the district of the Old Cemetery, and it was risky because you had to stoop to let the coffins pass under the branches and to lean the big crucifix, which wasn't a good idea because the nails were a little loose and the arms of the Christ had wobbled enough to create a small crack that was making them come loose from the body, like One-Arm's wooden elbow, and there was the danger that the Christ would fall in the mud, an enormous and irreparable sacrilege, like the one provoked by Fatso when on the occasion of his wife's death he wanted to take communion though he was dead drunk and as a result vomited the Host in the middle of the church, and the priest with a hop skip and a jump of vindictive rage came swooping down on him and shoving the onlookers aside cleared a space and in that space, sobbing on the floor on his knees and elbows, he labored with great delicacy around the Host until he isolated it, and while everyone knelt in a circle except for the husky fellows in the Confraternity who grabbed hold of Fatso who was still staggering around and kicked his ass out of the church, the priest had a clean handkerchief brought and a piece of white tissue paper, which he blessed and then passed the paper under the Host and sobbing transferred it with august respect to the handkerchief and from there to the altar. Fatso had this awful habit of profaning everything, even the cemetery, and when after a rainstorm the cross made of two sticks on his wife's grave was found broken everyone thought it was the storm, but the sexton knew it had been Fatso who every so often at night, especially when the wine ran out of his eyes in the form of tears, climbed over the hedge of the cemetery and crouched over his wife's grave as though to sleep beside her. Convinced of the danger of great sacrileges that would rebound on his conscience, the count gave the village a quarter of a field to have a new cemetery in a more central location, even though no one knows what the center of a village laid out in such a way would be, and so the Old Cemetery was immediately deconsecrated and the villagers held a meeting in the public square to deliberate about whom to give it to, and after democratic discussion they decided in favor of the Rapacinas. Old Rapacina planted wheat in it but the baker refused to make bread with the flour that came out of it, since it contained the blood of our dead, and no one wanted to buy it when the village philosopher and man of letters explained that if we eat the flesh of our ancestors, when the moment comes for the Resurrection of the flesh we'll be reborn incomplete because, God damn it, that flesh either has to stay with us or return to our ancestors.

Here in our village funerals are always held in the evening as the last light is fading and the darkness coming on, and sometimes even later, especially during the season when important work cannot be neglected or postponed. Death is something that burdens the mind and sinks like a probe into everyone's memory, old people and women and children, because as soon as someone dies the bells toll in long spaced intervals and the field hands working in scattered groups hear them and raise their heads and look each other in the face, and one will say, old Drugo's dead, or Bissaro, but another will correct him, it's la Traviata, or la Onta, or la Nana, or la Ronceta, and until the news is official and confirmed, all the old and sick people in the various districts are made to die in turn, and naturally they're the ones most anxious to find out the truth, above all so as to ward off, if only for a few days, the death that looms over their heads. The one who regularly hears the news first after the priest is Julia Imbroja because the priest himself sends her to tell it, whereupon la Imbroja, mistress of the situation, sets out wearing a black dress with a black veil and with the black book under her arm and goes to the house where the deceased lies exposed in the room closest to the entrance, and here one by one she rouses the dazed relatives and gives instructions and sends them to the grocer to buy long candles and to rent tall candlesticks and funeral sheets and to call the young women of the association, especially this or that individual who didn't show up last time, and when everything is ready she has them lay the deceased out in the center of the room under a sort of canopy and lines the walls with black gauze and lights the candles on the four candlesticks at the four corners of the corpse and all of a sudden begins intoning the rosary at the top of her lungs, to which the girls respond in semi-choruses, and recites the prayers and special formulas repeating them endlessly from dawn to dusk, with a brief interruption at noon to nibble a little cheese rind. As a result, after this delicate and painful moment, these litanies, in the minds of the family members, who have spent hours together watching over a dying person, enduring the parabola of death to its peak, and then some, to climb the slope again by clinging to such small ministrations as removing the polenta stuck between the dead man's teeth by holding his mouth open with one hand and with the other rubbing his gums with a twig, or better still, cleaning the corners of his eyelids with a handkerchief dampened with spit, or taking something to eat to the children who in their fear have stayed upstairs in the loft, I say these litanies, which go on until nine o'clock at night, are like a landslide sweeping them away and plunging them back into grief, and so it is that death crouches before them in the dirty image of a clumsy and embarrassing beast; it increases the children's fear and for two days they don't get out of bed. In the evening the dead man is taken to the church, at the center of a wailing procession, and people along the way take off their hats and stand aside, and it's even better if they fall in the ditch, as a sign of respect. The coffin is covered in the middle of the church with a gleaming black and silver cloth. During the ceremony the priest, prancing in his multicolored vestments around the coffin, intones, with broad gestures specified and regulated by the music of the organ, the Dies Lire, as we call it, that is to say he demands an accounting, and this obscure threat weighs heavily, like another imminent and incalculable misfortune, on the congregation, in which each sees himself already dead, and woe to anyone who touches his woman that night: a werewolf could be born, as may happen to those who conceive during the holy week of Advent.

When a woman conceives a child the shameful news is

kept secret as long as possible, and when her swelling belly reveals it to everyone the woman secludes herself to work in dark rooms, or is sent into the fields alone so that no one will notice if she has to vomit. She may set out in the morning before sunrise with her broad-brimmed straw hat and old trousers, because now it's no longer the way it was ten years ago when if the priest saw a woman in pants he covered his eyes with his hands and stamped his feet and la Imbroja would go trotting up behind her and call her a whore. On Sunday in church the pregnant woman so as not to be noticed will look for a little place to sit on the children's side, they being confined to special wooden benches because they don't have the five lire for a chair and besides they fight every so often and use dirty words, so it's better they be within range of the priest who with a hop skip and a jump comes down the steps of the altar like a bird of prey, grabs the luckless kid who's come out with a swear word in too loud a voice by the ear, drags him howling to the altar, makes him kneel on the first step, and gives him a violent rap on the noggin that sends him sprawling to kiss the marble, and the altar boys acquire rights over this mangy dog and because they're good can hit him on the head with the bell, and meanwhile the women turn around to look at the mother of this little pig, who in her shame draws her shawl to cover even her eyes and bowing her disheveled head gets ready to settle accounts with her scamp of a son. Then when the pregnant woman is starting to have labor pains, they send for the midwife who at first refuses but then has the obligation to come, because among other things the municipality gives her two bicycle tires a month gratis, and when she arrives she summons the other women, boils water, brings coals to heat the room, ties the noose of warm silk to the beams to hang the newborn baby by the feet and revive it with slaps if it's asphyxiated, and sends away all the men, who anyway are clumsy and of no use at all. They go rambling off in their cloaks through the fog, deciding they'll enter the first house they see illuminated and there study the omens, the cry of the owl, for instance, or the package of salt that tips over by itself, or the spider that comes out from under the polenta and crawls across the table among the dishes while they all watch it pleased and gratified, convinced that at that moment a boy was born because a spider at night brings good luck while a spider in the morning brings misfortune. Once the child is born it has to be immediately baptized, in the village church if it's born at home, while if it's born in the hospital, where however a woman can only go if everything is on the up and up, because Casimira, for example, who was pregnant but with no husband got a good slap in the face from the chief physician in person, then it's baptized in the cathedral in Montagnana, which you can immediately see is the work of the same architect who built the Kremlin, as they tell you in books. The mother, doubly unclean because she's been with a man and has held an unbaptized creature in her belly, is made to wait outside with a candle in her hand and if she sticks her nose in the door to see what's going on, the sacristan runs to close it, only at the end will she be admitted and allowed to walk not on carpets through the middle of the church but head bowed along the perimeter hugging the wall, and she and her child will be purified with the impressive words, uttered with upraised arms, go away, I exorcise you, unclean spirit, and at this point if you look closely you can see the baby wriggling and getting agitated because the devil is putting up a little useless resistance as though he didn't want to get out but to stay lodged inside there with his arms in its arms and his legs in its legs and his eyes in its eyes, but in the end the priest carefully makes the sign of the cross and at that moment the door of the church slams three times because the devil has gone roaming out over the fields to give vent to his anger.

So the years went by and those who had been old found themselves dead, those who had been young found themselves old, and those who hadn't been there before found themselves alive. Mother Crua had never opened her mouth except to drink a mug of thin broth prepared by her daughters with some mashed skinless beans, and the day when she didn't open her mouth even to drink no one was concerned since it had happened before and if you just had a little patience the old woman would always come round by herself and without being asked open her mouth to receive her soup, sometimes sitting there with her lips parted for half a day if no one was at home. Her daughter had made a sort of funnel out of cardboard to pour the liquid down her throat since the old woman didn't open her mouth more than a crack, into which it was impossible to stick the spoon. But after two days Mother Crua was still there, sitting on the cane chair, with her triangular head that looked like the caricature of a horse, and she gave no sign of moving. Worst of all, she stank. The youngest daughter went to call the Mouse, who before taking care of the old woman had been looking after the little girl, yes indeed, let's call her a little girl, because after all she wasn't a puppy, poor thing, who'd been born to the Crua girl and looked just like her in every respect, but even though resembling her entirely, in some ways she repeated the features of her grandmother, especially in the little eyes and in the tiny mouth that really looked too small to be good for anything, and it almost appeared as though the baby had been born with her head all closed up and with no openings like an oval squash, and that a surgeon with a scalpel had made two little cuts to open peepholes for the eyes, which fortunately were there underneath, and a little hole so the throat, which was functioning on its own, could breathe, and then, not knowing what to do about the ears, had detached a strip of skin on each side, but which in forming a scar had become shriveled and twisted like a little branch of coral. As soon as the Mouse came in the door, he noticed for the first time, and with a disgust that brought phlegm to his throat and made him turn his head and spit a great gob of saliva, that the Crua girl had acquired a remarkable resemblance to her mother, that her head, for instance, had become flattened and enlarged like an aluminum skillet battered and dented from being put too often on the fire, that her hair, partly by its nature and partly through dirt and indifference, was as sticky and tangled as tow, and her stomach was swollen and flabby, as happens toward the middle of life to those who have never had enough to eat. To be sure, it wasn't yet a stomach that sagged like a skirt as did that of her mother, whose legs seemed not to be attached to her belly but bundled inside it; a few decades of life, however, still remained to the Crua girl, and she would spend them sitting there on the chair, and end by adapting herself to it like mortar applied to a hole. With repugnance, the Mouse took hold of Mother Crua's hand and it was as though he had squeezed the hand of a marble statue, bloodless and absolutely hard, or with a wooden one, all cracked and with peeling and pustular bark. Then the Mouse forced open the old woman's mouth, and to the great satisfaction of the daughter inserted the funnel and poured in a little soup; the soup, to the daughter's great distress, came back out of the old woman's mouth and dribbled on her apron. Mother Crua had been dead for two days. The Mouse took her by the armpits and the daughters by the legs and deposited her on a blanket on the floor. Then the Mouse measured the dead woman's corpse by pacing the length of it and went to the carpenter to order the coffin, the eldest daughter went to the priest to arrange for the funeral, and the middle daughter disappeared. Only the youngest remained, there next to the decaying body, and she didn't know what to do. Finally she sat down in the chair that had been her mother's, made herself comfortable by shifting her buttocks to find the right position, and to the little girl, yes indeed, let's call her that since our language still doesn't have exact words for these people, she made a sign to indicate the feather brush.

1968-71

Author's note

When I had already finished a first draft of this book, I came into possession of a series of eyewitness accounts of the events in Part Two, taken down directly from the surviving participants. Where the two truths, mine and that of the witnesses, have coincided, I have sometimes preferred to yield the floor to them, with the result that in the finished version there are chapters consisting in part of the speech of others, inserted wherever it seemed to me appropriate in this attempt at a sort of nonfiction novel.

The chapters in Part Two thus become, at several points, a historical document, but I should emphasize that the little stories interwoven throughout the book, to create the background against which the main plot unfolds, are also true and not imaginary, while as a rule any resemblance to the real names of persons and places is accidental.

The event that destroyed the form of civilization depicted in the books *The Fifth Estate* and *Life Everlasting* was the arrival of the electric light, which occurred in the 1960's, and the almost simultaneous advent of television. But I wanted to recount, through the real fables that go to make up this "cycle of the lowest," not the dissolution of that civilization but how it functioned and persisted for a human eternity: its long "silence" and its brief "cry."

This book was designed by Austryn Wainhouse.
It was typeset by Stevens Graphics, of Brattleboro,
Vermont, and printed by McNaughton & Gunn, Inc.,
of Ann Arbor, Michigan.